IN FORMATION
20 Years Of Joda

José Montoya

© 1992 Chusma House Publications. All rights reserved. No part of this publication may be reproduced in any manner without permission in writing, except in the case of brief articles and reviews.

Publisher
Charley Trujillo, Chusma House Publications

Editors
Arturo Villarreal / Margarita Maestas-Flores

Alvarez Design & Illustration
Hiram Duran Alvarez

Typesetting
Linda Alvarez

Cover Art
José Montoya

Second Printing
Printed in Aztlán
ISBN: 0-9624536-1-7
Library of Congress
Catalog Card Number: 91-76195

CHUSMA HOUSE PUBLICATIONS

CONTENTS

PREFACE VIII

INTRODUCTION X

1969

Pobre Viejo Walt Whitman..........................1
El Vendido 2
Sunstruck While Chopping Cotton 3
Lazy Skin...4
In a Pink Bubble-Gum World 5
Los Vatos...6
La Jefita...9
Resonant Valley..11
La Cantinera De Stockton 13
El Louie 14

1971

Forgive?...17
Prawns For a mayan Princess.....................19

1972

Early Pieces...20
This Valley in September 21
"Jesse"..22
Misa en Fowler 23
From '67 to '71...24
The Hour Is Today 25
Valor y Locura..26
Jack-Off Hangover 27
Irish Priests and Chicano Sinners 28
Rabia 29

Esque Se Va Morir Don Chema...................30
Morir de Susto 31
Summer Soon Sunday Afternoon 32
My My!...33
Los Campos de Corcorán 34
X — mas '71 35
Monterey..36
Oh y Oh..37
Torres..38
S — Street y La Cinco del Barrio................39
La Muerte de un Gato 40
El Sol y Los de Abajo 41
A Moco Pome..44
Sisters and Brothers of Confusion..............45
Vamos a Dar la Vuelta 47
'61 Summer of Love 48
Metamorphosis — or, Guilty With an
Explanation 49
Gabby Took the 99 50

PORTFOLIO I

Mother Earth 52
La Chicana — y su Belleza...........................56
La Chicana — y su Fuerza 60
Heir to 500 years of Resistance 65

1973

Faces at the First Farmworkers Contitutional
Convention...72
Fiery Roses 77

The Guard Tower at the Consumnes
Correctional Center 78
The Form of a Kiss 79
La Gina 80
Pacheco Pass 81
Barrio Landmark 83
The Melancholia of Being a Poet at
Christmas Time 84
Late Autumn 85
At Forty, huevos and Pride Can Leave
You Dead 86
Purple Moon Over Portland Town 87
La Reina Mancornadora 88
Se fue Ricardo 89

1974

Five, Alone 90
Lay-over in Mazatlán —
One Year to the Day 92
El Tandito del Angelo 93
Always Do As You Are Told the
Best Way You Know How 94
The Movement Has Gone For Its Ph.D.
Over At the University,
Or the Gang Wars Are Back 95
Don't Ever Lose Your Driver's License ... 97
Una Lágrima por tu Amor 98
Orito del Barrio con Safos 99
The People's Representative 100
El Barrio en enero 101

Tres Cantos en Vano 102
Arroz Is Arroz Is Arroz 104
A Happy Dog Is 107

1975

The Faceless Wonder 108
The Grain Shed 109
Hotel Royalty 110
El Padre Nuestro and the Park 112
The Barrio Artist/Teacher 114
Until They Leave Us a Loan 115

1976

You Know I Wouldn't if Only
I Could Masturbate 118
El Veterano 119
. . . . a poem with the title at the end ... 121
Faltan Quince Pa' las Cuatro 122
Two Letters 123
They Sent Men to Match Mountains ... 124
La Yarda de la Escuelita 126
Eslipping and Esliding 129
Yore's Days 131
The Paradox of Loneliness 132
Mujer Sin Fe 133
Soledad 134

PORTFOLIO II

Pachucos 136
Cholos 144
Juntitos los Dos 152

Wars and Warriors 156

1977
Los Theys Are Us 161
In the Gaze of a Black Eagle 163
Under the Shade of a Fruitless
Mulberry Tree 165
Beautiful Performance at Evening Time 167

1980
The River 168
The Carrión Eaters 170
Listen 171

1981
The Telling Signs of Downtown 172
Un Canto de Amor Sereno 174

1982
Renovation of the State Capitol 175
Dennis Is Risen In Celebration 176

1983
How Great Was My Valley 177

1985
El Sol y 'L Rovato Loco 178
A Day of Infamy 179
Twin Double-Barrel Shotgun 180
In Lak 'Ech on the Rocks 181

1986
Rough Time in th' Barrio 182

Rain 183
Th' Dog Dreamers 184
Albert Camus' Roach-Clip or
Sysiphus Con Muleta 185
Dress Down 186

PORTFOLIO III
Blind Faith 188
Humor 192
Mask of Oppression 196
La Joda y La Lucha Continua 204

1987
A Way of Life — A Way of Death 212
Cinco de Mayo Poem for '87 213
Where's Your Face, Ace? 215
One Casindio's Reaction to the Media 216

1988
Crack 217
A Cleansing/Una Limpiada 220
The Xura Cura Tribe Reports 221
Aun 226
The Uniform of the Day 228

1989
Hispanic Nightlife at Luna's Cafe When
Th' Mexicans Came to Visit th'
Chicanos in Califas 230
A Chicano Veterano's War Journal 232

1990
Pachuco Portfolio 233

The Songs y Los Corridos
Garbanzo Beret 235
Lulac Cadillac 236
Los Huelguistas 237
Derelict Dawg 238
El Marinero Mariguano 239
El Rosinante 241
Cruzin' 243
Big Momma 244
Pesadilla Yanqui 245
Arpa Chicana 246
El Tirilongo 247
Chicanos en Korea 248
El Billy Billy Militante 250

Acknowledgements Continued 251

GRACIAS

First and foremost, le doy su muy mercído lugar a mi querida esposa Juanita por su apoyo y su paciencia. Muchas gracias a mi familia for their incredible patience y por su apoyo. Thanks from the heart a mi carnala de lucha desde el año del pan duro, Olivia Castellano, for her faith in my word forging. Special thanks to Lorna Dee Cervantes (and her manguitos) for early on seeing the need for "information". For all their hard work and dedication in making sure this project was done, very special thanks to Gina, my daughter, y las future poetisas de CLLA, Chicana Latina Literary Association, de CSUS: María Mejorado, Leticia Bermúdez, María Chacón y Aída Molina. They inspire their mentors! And to the latest "Wings" to our squadron of adobe airplanes — third generation Royal Chicano Air Force astro pilots of Aztlán: Felipe Magdaleno, Chuey Barela, Abran Robles, Jesse Areano y Rubén Lerma, de la ala, Los Adaces; and Mario Moreno, José Chico Lott, Margarita Magdaleno, Pasqual Márquez, Andrea Porras, Emilio Soltero, Louie Louie García, David Buenrostro and Joe Rodríguez, of the Impudent Young Pilots wing — to both groups, I want to thank for las canas que le han sacado aquí al profe and for the memories de aquéllas parrandas que no terminamos. Sincere gratitude to El Maestro, Rudy Carrillo, for steering the course del Trío Casindio. Finally, with love and respect, thanks to all the plebe del RCAF and to all my relations! Ho.

— *José Montoya*

PREFACE
Twenty Years Of Joda, With Love

At 58, th' weight of a tremendous load begins to settle, altering one's bearing. Eventually that load will come to represent the sum of all th' past experience in one's journey upon this earth, however varied. Lo bueno y lo malo.

The bizarre an' th' sublime. The whole enchilada begins to settle, sagging the carriage un escante. And you realize you have to carry it. You can't unload it, so you balance it. At 58, it is at once an exhilarating time — My God, I rose to those occasions? And it is also the most excruciatingly painful of times — to face the reality that one has at times stooped lower than levels of human decency should allow. But memory can be manipulated. It allows denial as well as illumination. Que grocera y que dulce la memoria — candy and bile all the while! But at 58, the returns are coming in. The load leadens. Time to shift the weight. Sharing helps, but only up to a point. The mental load can be absorbed by the physical, and the mind can ease the physical hurt.

And so, aquí con esta obra, I can take the cuerno by the horns, swallow my pride, bite my tongue, lower my chompeta y me sanbuto right up-almost-to-the-hilt, in order to ease the burden. So I hereby share with my people the memory of 20 years of joy, 20 years of joda. Time to unload and begin preparing for the next 20. La resistencia continues. Got to move light. Y sigue la bola. Love and struggle ain't just for 20 years, es por vida. Ho.

Xoda?

And about this word, JODA? Well, I was warned, and the fun has already begun. The term is tripping both the practitioners of Spanish and the non-practitioners. I originally wanted to use the word chinga, but its verb form has already been aptly treated by the much admired and respected Mexican poet/philosopher, Octavio Paz. Besides, for my purposes, joda seems better suited to describe struggle and resistance than chinga, that is if the word is used right. Watch 'em try to sound the "J" like "jay," which makes it joda, pronounced Jowda. Sounds too much like chora, barrio slang for phallus. And yora sounds like a lament, which is close; but it is simply joda, like in jodidos — which brings up the "H" sound — 'odidos?

Odiados, perhaps, especially by some of our own Chicanistas attempting to fit the joya que es nuestra cultura into Eurocentric paradigms, like stuffing ancestral bones into glass cases for museums. It can be done but shouldn't. So, in that sagrada joya jodida, Chicanos discover love — a gem-stone called culture, which unlike the rock of Sisyphus, carries us up and down the hill. Y seguimos jodiendo until que los jodidos nos oigan. Ho!

Tres Portfolios Chicanos From/For The 4 Directions

Regarding the art work, each portfolio contains four categories illustrating significant aspects of the love and joda, inherent in and crucial to the Chicano worldview. They were drawn on napkins, paper towels, toilet seat covers, and even toilet paper. Whatever was available during rare respites of the last twenty years. They were done in bars, restaurants, laundromats, on the road, and in jail houses. I chose to include 'em because they were done en el mismo espíritu that the poems were written.

The Songs y Los Corridos

The songs and the corridos are included in the book because these too were written as the move meant to go during those twenty years. Organizing is never easy. Art es joda. Poetry, painting, teaching — pure joda! Flying adobe airplanes is double joda. You need a song now and again to elevate the spirit, and then all the joda becomes jubilation. So we wrote songs, and we sang them. In the marches, en los files/filas/fields an' city halls and halls of just us, ese! Tamanio tamborzón el corazón! Chicano power! Chicano powder keg and power plays — con el Che y La Virgen por delante — singing. Singing.

INTRODUCTION
Valor y Locura: The Poetic Space of José Montoya

Thirty-three thousand feet above the vast Atlantic, in a plane cruising at 600 miles an hour, confronted with the fragility of my life, I began to understand the space where José Montoya has lived during these twenty years of struggle. Perched high above the abyss, armed with only "sentimientos, valor y locura" and with his visions etched on his soul like the paintings of Goya — this poet has led an impeccable and courageous life. With healthy fatalism his jefitos taught him as they swam up and down the migrant stream from New Mexico to Califas, rendered razor-sharp by oppression and betrayal, relentless in his optimism that his people will make it, and on their own terms — this RCAF pilot-poet has survived and is coming in for a landing.

In his own deconstruction of "Joda," José explains how he first thought of using "chinga" in the title of this much-awaited book (his second after EL SOL Y LOS DE ABAJO AND OTHER POEMS). But "chingar," unlike "joder," implies loss and passivity while the latter signifies action, effort, and tireless commitment to the "lucha." Translating "jo-da" in classic-Montoya style, he is quick to point out that it also means "Joe-gives." Without faltering and without being compliant, he surrendered himself completely to the Chicanos' quest for dignity and cultural survival. I am reminded of Juan Bruce-Navoa's statement in his masterful analysis of "El Louie":

"Life is to be judged in terms of class, not what is done but how, which equals life as an aesthetic act." [1]

In the twenty-two years I have known my friend, colleague, and camarada, José Montoya, I can only say that the vato's life has been remarkable.

These poems, spanning the years from 1969 to 1989, are his brunt offering, a magnificent gift that José has given us. He offers them humbly, without pretense or affectation, just as he has lived his life. It is impossible to separate the man from the poet. This is the work of a man who has given selflessly of his time, energy, and love to la gente, la causa del campesino y el movimiento cultural y artistico de la gente Chicana. Through it all he has never doubted that the struggle has been worthwhile "La lucha es útil." Make no mistake, his has not been blind optimism. He is aware that annihilation threatens his people on a daily basis and that destruction can, and often does, come from within. Herein lies the wonderful contradiction of Montoya's poetic voice: hope in the face of desperation, beauty amidst squalor, joy in the face of tragedy.

The best poets have always concerned themselves with the contradictions in the human experience. As a Chicano poet, Montoya has found a particularly rich vein of contradiction and paradox in his own life, the Chicano experience and life in general. This is the predominant pattern which unifies IN FORMATION: TWENTY YEARS OF JODA. And, as the poet-persona of "El Sol y Los de Abajo" reminds us:

> Como raises de granos enterrados—
> Esos son los pensamientos que
> Llevo — contradictions and
> Paradoxes — that I'm not so
> Sure I want to set straight. . .

When the plane lands, I can best appreciate the real space of his poetry, the theater of tension, a powerful drama in which the poet has cast his people as his collective hero. He shows us, on the one hand, the stark, hard reality that characterizes the Chicanos' life in the United States. On the other hand, he captures the spirit of their invincibility. He is at once the hard-core realist and the romantic idealist (as he reminds his beautiful daughter Gina in the poem that bears her name: "De mi sacastes/a penchant for the ideal/and the romantic").

At the core of his book is this motif of contradiction. He is at once a gentle poet and the powerful socio-political satirist; the vato-loco-derelict-dog stand-up comic, and yet the philosophical poet who can write sympathetically about la jefita and los niños en la escuelita at the foot of the sierra in New Mexico. Montoya is nostalgic for a simpler past yet very much in the here and now. His feet are firmly rooted in the earth (la madre tierra) yet he is always flying high above, in formation, threatening to deliver a powerful indictment against this conformist, blind society.

In his effusiveness and cosmic vision, he brings to mind Walt Whitman, the grey poet. However, this brown Chicano poet celebrates his people in starker and more powerful terms. In his stylistic versatility, Montoya more closely resembles Pablo Neruda, especially Neruda's early surrealist period and his later socio-political reformist poetry.

Like Whitman and Neruda, Montoya is the workingman's poet. He eloquently reminds us in "El Sol y Los de Abajo," how he dragged himself through the morass of poverty and oppression which characterizes the life of the downtrodden, the misbegotten:

> . . . Soy de los de
> Abajo — find the gutters
> The prisons, the battlefields,
> Y los files de algodón —
> Ahi me encuentran. En las vecindades . . .

Dressed in his baggies, Pendleton shirt, and Stetson Beaver hat, or his blue Sir Guy jacket and watch cap for colder weather, this people's poet, in his non-conformist professor's 'uniform of the day', reaches deep within the poet's bag of madness and magic to find:

> . . . a poem
> For the damaged dream
> As beautiful as the one
> For the dream fulfilled.
>
> *("Albert Camus 'Roach-Clip or Sisyphus Con Muleta")*

And indeed, Once you embrace a people to the point that you personify them, as José personifies Chicanos, your heart will be broken upon seeing so many damaged dreams. In the poem "Los Vatos," he sings the song of lament; mourns for young vatos like Benny, killed by his own camaradas after last night's dance; Louie, who dies alone in a rented room after having been the barrio's local hero in "El Louie"; Gabby, who leaves the campesino's lifestyle only to die of an overdose in Viet Nam. Then there's the three young Chicanos who die in vain: Roger, the ex-Beret, dead at twenty-six; the Big Brown Buffalo, dead at twenty-two; and Tony, who felt death was the finest high because you only do it once, "Tres Cantos en Vano." He also grieves for Dennis, for whom only a cooing dove sings a dirge, "Dennis Is Risen in Celebration."

To be sure, there is much to lament in these twenty years of struggle. In "Sunstruck While Chopping Cotton," he moves to a different level and shows us the destruction of our planet, i.e., the Long Beach waters where the Bothisattvas, young novice monks who are trying to save the world, enter and get cut down by surfboards sharp as razors or get entangled in oil-well derricks. From the shade of a mulberry tree, the poet-persona watches with a weary eye the daily attempts at survival of "el barrio oprimido." In "The Telling Signs of Downtown," he holds up to us the disturbing images of the inner-city homeless, starving, huddled like phantoms, hunch-shouldered against the cold, trekking from park to park, looking for a place to sleep. In "The Guard Tower at the Consumes Correctional Center," he reminds us that the people who often end up in jail are "scores of martyred Raza, political Blacks," and addicted children, along with their "derelict fathers." He condemns, in "Renovation of the State Capitol," the phallic dome of government, which is thrusting itself into the sky, advertising its love of lies and gold.

The poet lashes out with contempt. His work is a serious indictment against the way society has dealt with its poor and with the environment. In "How Great Was My Valley," he shows us a variation of the "greying of America" metaphor: grey cropdusters, grey silos and barns, water towers, mist, ashes, and poisoned grass. He wonders how hawks in the grey sky manage to outnumber cropdusters.

He also ridicules the distorted priorities of a society that places minor importance on education and cultural achievement. This is conveyed most memorably in "Rough Time in the Barrio." When funds are cut off for his barrio art class, Luisita, one of his elderly student artists, brings him a brown bag containing U.S. Government surplus butter and cheese, with the gentle reminder not to worry because all will work out in the end. But Luisita captures the unmistakable optimism which runs right alongside the poet's lament. He does not allow himself to be overcome by the images he paints with such photographic clarity. While the outcry is clear and the condemnation strong, the poet is able to find beauty amidst squalor, strength in the face of impending doom. Even when Montoya is describing the saddest scenes and events, there lingers a trace of hope. It comes from his ability to see what we cannot see, appreciate what we overlook. Although la jefita is making tortillas in the squalor of a labor camp hut, her beans boil musically on the stove and almost triumph above the nocturnal sounds of the campesino's world. In "Resonant Valley," he captures the irony of being called lazy though his family are "quinienteros," who can finish 500 trays of produce with the day barely two thirds along. And the "Cantinera de Stockton," despite her work as barmaid and hints at an older, "nobler" profession, is a virgin without equal, because her innocence and goodness are genuine. Rosa, the cantinera in "Early Pieces," who reads funnybooks and "lifts her dress a little" for the curious pre-adolescent boys, brings to mind the large, earthly woman in Fellini's AMACORD, who lives alone by the sea, having lost touch with reality. Like Rosa, she is both tempting and frightening in her raw sensuality.

"The Barrio Artist Teacher" captures the joy of working with non-traditional students — stone vatos locos caressing clay, a child of poverty whose eyes light up as he explores the potentiality of his own inner artist's world and the ancianos who, with wrinkled smiles and gnarled fingers, are able to forget the pain of aging as they work the clay. Only the kiss of a wino, schooled in the art of loneliness, can ease the poet's personal sorrow in "Barrio Landmark."

Poems in which the tone is most uplifting are those in which the poet is simply describing. Witness, for example, the sun doing battle with the fog and winning in "El Padre Nuestro and the Park" (which he dedicates to Juanishi Orozco). Or, the gorgeous theatrics of nature in the "Beautiful Performance at Evening Time." Here, the eye of the poet and that of the artist come together exquisitely. Note his description of the cloud configurations; he sees first a boat, then white and grey stallions, now a beautiful bride. While these poems demonstrate Montoya's fascination with images, those like "La Yarda de la Escuelita" illustrate his aural gift as well, his ear finely tuned to the sounds of school children during recess. He captures this virtually all in Spanish. No other Chicano- living poet today knows how to extract the alliterative richness of the Spanish language as Montoya can:

> Alrededor de la maestra
>
> Acurrucadis de miedo — como pollitos —
>
> Se amontonan los del baby room
>
> Asustados desde Setiembre

And, later when the bell rings and the children return from recess:

> Convergen los niños a matacaballo
>
> Riendo y gritando
>
> Gritando y unos llorando
>
> Tropesandose y puchando,
>
> Acabando con todo.

Montoya's linguistic genius is most evident in poems like "La Jefita" and "El Louie," in which he plays with the sound boundaries between English and Spanish to create a species of Caló, a language all his own. No one but Montoya can capture the heavy bilingual, Caló-laden voice of Eliás, alias Eelye, in "Until They Leave Us A Loan," especially when Eelye explains how he and the rest of the Chicanada took over McKinley Park one summer.

> Y luego despues, que curada,
>
> Watcha — we used to ride around
>
> The park en Mercs y Chevies,
>
> Tu sabes — and C 2 pistols

> In the back seat — just circling
> The pinche park, como guardias,
> Dig? Drinking Ripple, white
> And red, and for the rucas
> Pagan Pink.

Evidence of Montoya's poly-lingustic artistry abounds in the annals of Chicano literary criticism. "La Jefita" and "El Louie" are, without doubt, the two most celebrated poems in Chicano literature to date.

To seek the source of the contradiction, the core paradox in the poet's larger concern, one must look at poems like "Los Theys Are Us," in which he speaks of betrayal as coming from within. He admonishes us, reminding us that "We were once a principled people. Ser chuecos was never our style." Now, unfortunately, we have lost our integrity, our respect for each other. In "The Xura Cura Tribe Reports," he is angered when Chicano intellectuals denigrate the work of a Chicana at international literature conferences. Annihilation can, and often does add wariness to the poet's persona. Throughout the poetic act, his eyes are open. His are not flights of fancy; his love is not uncritical.

What to do in the face of such a dilemma? How to handle the singular knowledge that his people, in addition to living under the constant threat of cultural, spiritual, and economic oblivion, must also protect themselves from each other? How does one maintain the "Cockroach Integrity Intact" if one must live in that precarious world, caught between two cultures belonging to neither? This "casi" or "sin" home dialectic he poignantly captures in "Aún," his excellent treatise on the demands of living between different cultures while trying to carve out space one can call home.

When the spirit is forced to live under siege, how does it cope? For part of the answer, one must turn to poems like "Eslipping and Eslidding," where he explains how the spirit develops a certain courage, "Valor y Locura," the ability to laugh at oneself, controlled insanity. From this ability (coupled with one's impeccability or the way one has spent the days shifting and shuffling and coping with oppression) comes the will to survive. Insanity finally convinces us that the struggle has been worthwhile.

This type of madness reaches full fruition in his insanely imaginative poems like "Th' Dog Dreamers," which are Daliesque in their surrealism. These poems, along with his derelict-dog poems, are best appreciated when considered in connection with his PACHUCO BARRIO DOG paintings. These are not whiny, pampered dogs but hard-core, veterano pitbulls who can kick ass in the Barrio — wise, confident dogs, scarred survivors of the barrio struggle. Only in this context can we appreciate the full surrealistic impact of:

> A mean-mouthed pack of dogs
> Came out of stage left
> Moving across America . . .
> In rapacious slow motion

The dogs appear and evanesce, fading in and out across the poet-persona's line of vision. The first dog is a 'shadow-cloud spectre', the second is transparent; but the third:

> Wore zoot suit pants
> And shades — tea-timers
> to hide the white of his red eyes
> It appeared
> and spoke to the house
> With the tile roof.

How else can one understand the derelict dog blues and the dog that smiles as it comes around the corner?

Insanity gives us vision and courage to defy the monster of every threatening chaos. Controlled insanity is the space where the poet and artist in Montoya come together. This is what it means to fly IN FORMATION: to care so much that you no longer care, love so much that you no longer love (Shantih, Shantih — T.S. Eliot).

High above the Atlantic, reading his poetry at that altitude, I became fearless and allowed myself to enter the poet's spirit. Once I did, the voices came keening, rushing at me in a frenzy — the voice of Eelye and Gabby, who dared to dream, las ancianas of the Barrio Art class, all the jefitas of the world, the howling derelict dogs, all the unorganizables at the first farmworkers' union meeting. The Sacra' homeless, the prisioneros, the cantineras, and the niños at play. All the voices of la gente, voices of struggle in all their tragedy, all their joy high up there, I could hear them in unison. The voices, Montoya's words, had become real. And, as Bruce Navoa reminds us:

> "This is the power of the word's appearance in the
> world: to represent an absence in such a convincing
> manner that the representation can actually become
> reality . . ." [2]

This is the power I feel when I read IN FORMATION: TWENTY YEARS OF JODA. I will say of this poetry what Pablo Neruda once said of Federico Garcia Lorca's : ". . . as time passes, the people with their marvelous intuition will claim his words, will sing them in their folk poetry." [3]

Montoya has given back to his people their voice. In the end the words, the power, will again be theirs. This book itself, alas, will belong to the critics. But I know they will miss the nopales, the campesinos, las viejitas, los vatos y las escuelitas — the whole map of every Chicano barrio etched into the face of every poem. The critics will see him from Derridean perspectives, tracing his signifiers and themselves, walking down with him "por toda la calle Efe," working alongside him en "Los Campos de Corcoran," and the fields of Sanger and Parlier. Both perspectives will be equally valid. One would expect no less from the vato whose life and work have been remarkable.

I burn the "juas" for you, compañero — for this book and many more to come. Ho!

— *Olivia Castellano*

Foot Notes

1. Juan Bruce-Nova, CHICANO POETRY: A RESPONSE TO CHAOS
   (Austin Tx.: University of Texas Press, 1982), p. 16.
2. Ibid., p.24
3. Pablo Neruda, PASSIONS AND IMPRESSIONS
   (ed. Matilde Neruda and Miguel Otero Silva) (New York: Farrar Straus and Giroux, 1980), p. 60.

Lovingly dedicated to the memory del manito mayor, great teacher and respected Chicano elder.

Cleofes Vigil
1917-1992

1969

POBRE VIEJO WALT WHITMAN

When the good grey poet
Imposed his virile image
Upon an impotent people no
Envisionó en su locura
Stoop-shouldered junkies
Aching to get straight and
Hip-swinging he-men
Abrazandose en callejones oscuros.
And now he reappears, much,
Much later in far-off Lhasa
Un monje solitario and he
Abhors the sight his third eye
Sees as he stirs the dying
Brasas of his dry yak dung fire
Which emits such little warmth.

Y volverá otra vez, again and again
Y con cada resurrección he
Shall shed reluctantly that
Self-adulation which led him,
Ciego, from the East River
To the singing hills of a
Land emasculating itself,
Dejando droppings of
Asphalt and reinforced concrete.

1969

EL VENDIDO

Blunt, dull pain
Like nothing
But, oh, yes
That lingers and
Envelops my soul

Like sack-cloth

Bequeathing penitence
Upon my sanguine hopes
Sorry remnants of
Once regal Dons
Yet earlier Yaquis

Vestiges fading fast

From the pain
That hurts my Raza
Concerned now
With boats in the
Driveway, the Boy Scouts

And the World Series

And I
The weakest
Condemned to bear
It all for reasons of
Betrayal only my father's

Dead father can fathom

And he died for Villa
That year of the
Revolution of pain
So much
Sweeter than

Mine.

SUNSTRUCK WHILE CHOPPING COTTON

It was at first a single image.
A mirage-like illusional dance
Wavering and decomposing in the
Distance like a plastic mosaic.

Then it cleared.

Not one but three Bothisattvas
Suspended in a cloud of yellow dust
Just above the rows of cotton
Galloping comically on skeletal mounts
Across the arid, sponge-like lust
Of a desiccated desert.

They ride by, shouting in ruthless unison
The name of Jesus, across the valley
Halting not for an instant in their trek
To the distant sea.

The cool sea.

With flame throwers for nostrils
Their horses flee
Abreast the three
Halting whole freeways of awe-stricken traffic
And scattering chattering choppers
Welcoming the enormous episode as an excuse
For frolic and fanfare.
They enter the sea and immediately get

Cut down by surf boards sharp as razors
And oil-well derricks entangle them
And the horses, not being divine, drown.
And the Bothisattvas, mountless in the mire
Choke and struggle, making the Long Beach
Waters thick with blood, mud, and crude oil.

But they are determined, and they walk
Nimbly and bloodied on the cracked-mirror
Surface with all the humility of the East.
Then they forget and break into a run
Leaving bloodied footprints upon the blue waters,
Running, running, toward the setting sun.

Shouting, Jesus saves!
In ruthless unison.

LAZY SKIN

Como
Imagen primordial
De las epocas
Más allá del pasado
Formulated by the Gaba

Who has used
It to strap,
Stifle, and
Almost convince
Me.

Reteniendo mis
Obras hidden in me
Pero desnudas a
Mis instintos.
Who, as I, feels

The weight of despair?
The weightlessness of
Exhilaration?
Ambiente —
Transparente como
Una jolla, opaca como
El carbon, heavy like
A feather — carga fija
Del hombre marginal.
Aflicción arquetipica
Reposando en los armarios

De mi mente — white imposed
Demented mannerism —
Time
Has exposed you!

And it begins to show
Now in the tested
Consequences of earlier
Hypothesis that pre-
Suppositions fueron

Nociones deseosas, sustaining
In me that impetus — como
Dijo el existencialista Danés,
The illness unto death —
Hope!

¡Olvidemos la esperanza!
¡Hechos, mi Raza!
¡Hechos!

1969

IN A PINK BUBBLE-GUM WORLD

Preso
Locked inside a glass-like
Canopy built of grief
And hurtings
Not entirely my own

WORDS!

But I have contributed
Porque soy pendejo
And I've mortared them
With self-pity!

¡A mi gente le importa mádre!

Do I believe it? I believe it!
I believe it! Do I believe it?
Believe! Believe! Believe!

¿Y qué nos queda, hermanitos?

To look out at a gravel path

Esperando al contratista.
Ahí viene el troque, hechen
Los sacos!

And even beyond, los divinos
With stereoscopic vision-pink

Peach blossoms — PINK!
Blooming in the distant
Gabacho spring.

Pero armado con estas palabras
De sueños forged into files —

"Las filas de la rebelion"
Cantaban los dorados de Villa.

I approach the casing.
The bubble gives ¡PERO no se
Rompe!

And dream tools fail to
Penetrate the placental shroud.

¡SOLO NO PUEDO, HERMANOS!

1969

LOS VATOS

Back in the early fifties, el Chonito and I were on the
Way to the bote when we heard the following dialogue:

Police car radio: Pachuco rumble in progress in front of Lyceum
    Theatre. Sanger gang crossing tracks heading for
    Chinatown. Looks big this time. All available
    Westside units . . .

Cop to partner driving car:
    Take your time. Let 'em wipe each other out.

    That attitude was typical then. Has it changed?

    Below I sing of an unfortunate act of that epoch.

They came to get him at three o'clock
On a Sunday afternoon that summer of '48.
Five of them and a guitar in a blue '37 Chevy.

    (The vatos always carried guitars and drove around
    In low Chevies with bad metallic paint jobs.)

Two got down soothing long, sleek hair,
Hidden eyes squinting behind green-tinted tea-timers.
In cat-like motions, bored and casual, they sauntered
Then settled heavily on the car.

The one called Chava whistled the familiar whistle
Which now sounded alien. The other drew a handkerchief,

1969

Squatted slowly and wiped his thick-soled shoes —
Twin mirrors of despair, reflecting a wine bottle
Making the rounds in gurgling sounds inside the car.

Benny watched them from the window of the tiny bedroom.
His little sister of the huge, slanting eyes — eyes that
Surely witnessed in another time, in another land now
Foreign, Moctezuma slain — played on the bed; life being
Still good to her at that age. But Benny felt sorry for
Himself by feeling sorry for her. He felt a numb sorrow
For many things — and he felt anger.

His brain, his stomach, his feet — all of him —
Was not himself at all, and he could stand outside
And look in. He was at once a rock and a lump of jello
Something — a thing, but not himself.

    This he could see and not understand fully, but
    Everything that was happening was happening, somehow.

"The boys!" called his mother, and her innocence
Made lacerations on his torpid mind. "Benito, the guys
Want you, ven! Cuidado, and don't stay out late!"
She warned, in false concern. Benny is a good boy!

He walked past her without seeing her and in his thoughts
Illusive like a moth, the incredible notion
To crawl into her and the chance to be born again
Passed before him.

1969

    But the street and the heat and the guys waited.

Like all the other times of camaraderie of long ago
Before last night's dance had changed all that
And now a mask went forth strutting a brave deathwalk
A clouded mind half-knowing, aware only of the hot sun's
Leaping flames bouncing off the Fresno street.

    He was consumed by a wall of heat and he managed
    To utter, "here?" Then the mercury burst!

And he felt a red-hot wire — or was it a piece of ice? —
Pass across his belly and he expired a soft moan of relief
Then his breath was cut short from behind —
Then again,
And again!

    And his mother came screaming.

1969

LA JEFITA

When I remember the campos
    Y las noches and the sounds
of those nights en carpas o
Bagones I remember my jefita's
    Palote
       Click-clok; clik-clack-clok
    Y su tocesita.

(I swear, she never slept!)

Reluctant awakenings a la media
Noche y la luz prendida.

      PRRRRRRRINNNNGGGGG!

A noisy chorro missing the
    Basín.

¿Que horas son, 'ama?
Es tarde mi hijito. Cover up
Your little brothers.
Y yo con pena but too sleepy,

    Go to bed little mother!

A maternal reply mingled with
The hissing of the hot planchas
Y los frijoles de la olla
Boiling musically, dando segunda

A los ruidos nocturnos and
The snores of the old man

    Lulling sounds y los perros
Ladrando — then the familiar
Hallucinations just before sleep.

    And my jefita was no more

But by then it was time to get up!

My old man had a chiflidito
That irritated the world to
Wakefulness.

    Wheeeeeeet! Wheeeeeeet!

¡Arriba, cabrones chavalos,
Huevones!

    Y todavia la pinche
    Noche oscura

Y la jefita slapping tortillas.

    ¡Prieta! Help with the lonches!
    ¡Calientale agua a tu 'apa!

(¡Me la rayo ese! My jefita never slept!)

1969

Y en el fil, pulling her cien
Libras de algoda se sonreía
Mi jefe y decía,

That woman — she only complains
In her sleep.

RESONANT VALLEY

When I was
Young among
The pregnant
Vineyards of
All the un-domed
Capitals of
The raisin
Industry —
Musically chiming
Charming towns like
Fowler
Reedley
Del Rey
Selma
Clovis
Parlier
Kingsburg and Sanger —

I was lazy

Me!

From a family
Of clean pickers
The pride of
Any Fijikawa or
Saroyanesque Krikor —

Quinienteros of

Five hundred trays
And the day barely
Two thirds along

But everyone said I was

Lazy.

I knew. But how I knew!

Why I was easy
On the clusters —
Careful with
The leaves,

Slow.

I was too quick to
Sadden at the sight
Of the green, iridescent worm
Scorching itself in the
Hot, planed-for-trays, sand.
And knowing I had something
To do with its death

I wept.

And rather than
Repeat the

1969

Senseless carnage
I remained lazy

Sitting under the vines
Imagining what my reactions
Would be to some similar
Onslaught.

Panic!

Intolerable panic!
With both
Hands
Upon my head
My eyes
Shut tight
Flashing
Stabs of color
On the roof
Of my skull — and
A child-young urge
To roll
Naked
Upon the burning sand,
I remained lazy.

And the family
Of quinienteros
Didn't make as much

Money
That summer
In the valley of the San Joaquin.

But the worms, the wasps, and the
Black widow spiders — for a short
Time, at least — frolicked
cooly in that green-leaf world

Beneath the sun.

LA CANTINERA DE STOCKTON

Virgin without equal
    because your
Innocence emits a
    quality too
Rare and a transcend-
    ing
Goodness so pure as to
    tarnish higher
Idols surely tainted
    otherwise, and your
Nymph-like movements
    contradict the
Immaculate completeness
    that envelops you.
Angel masquerading as a
    barmaid, your colorific
    shell appropriately
    deceives

EL LOUIE

Hoy enterraron al Louie.

And San Pedro o san pinche
Are in for it. And those
Times of the forties
And the early fifties
Lost un vato de atolle.

Kind of slim and drawn,
There toward the end,
Aging fast from too much
Booze y la vida dura. But
Class to the end.

En Sanjo you'd see him
Sporting a dark topcoat
Playing in his fantasy
The role of Bogart, Cagney,
Or Raft.

Era de Fowler el vato,
Carnal del Candi y el
Ponchi — Los Rodriguez —
The Westside knew 'em,
And Selma, even Gilroy.
'48 Fleetline, two-tone —
Buenas garras and always
Rucas — como la Mary y
La Helen . . . siempre con

Liras bien afinadas
Cantándo La Palma, la
Que andaba en el florero.

Louie hit on the idea in
Those days for tailor-made
Drapes, unique idea — porque
Fowler no era nada como
Los, 'ol E.P.T. Fresno's
Westside was as close as
We ever got to the big time.

But we had Louie, and the
Palomar, el boogie, los
Mambos y cuatro suspiros
Del alma y nunca faltaba
That familiar, gut-shrinking,
Love-splitting, asshole-up-
Tight, bad news —

    ¡Trucha, esos! Va 'ver
    Pedo!
    ¡Abusao, ése!
    Get Louie!

No llores, Carmen, we can
Handle 'em.
    ¿Ese, 'on tal Jimmy?
    ¿Órale, Louie!

1969

Where's Primo?
   ¡Va 'ver catos!
En el parking lot away from the jura
   ¡Órale!
   ¿Tráis filero?
   ¡Simón!
   ¡Nel!
   ¡Chále, ése!
   ¡Oooooh, este vato!

An Louie would come through —
Melodramatic music, like in the
Mono — tan tan tran! — Cruz
Diablo, El Charro Negro! Bogart
Smile (his smile as deadly as
His vaisas) He dug roles, man,
And names — like "Blackie," "Little
Louie . . ."

Ese Louie . . .
Chále, man, call me "Diamonds"!

Y en Korea fue soldado de
Levita con huevos and all the
Paradoxes del soldado razo —
Heroism and the stockade!
And on leave, jump boots
Shainadas and ribbons, cocky
From the war, strutting to

Early mass on Sunday morning.

Wow, is that 'ol Louie?

¡Mire, comadre, ahí va el hijo
De Lola!

Afterward he and fat Richard
Would hock their Bronze Stars
For pisto en el Jardín Canales
Y en El Trocadero.

At barber college he came
Out with honors. Después
Empeñaba su velardo de la
Peluca pa' jugar pocar cerrada
And lo ball en Sanjo y Alviso.

And "Legs Louie Diamond" hit
On some lean times . . .

Hoy enterraron a Louie.

Y en Fowler at Nesei's
Pool parlor los baby chukes
Se acuerdan de Louie, el carnal
Del Candi y el Ponchi — la vez
Que lo fileriaron en el Casa
Dome y cuando se catio con

1969

La Chiva.

Hoy enteraron al Louie.

His death was an insult
Porque no murió en acción —
No lo mataron los vatos,
Ni los gooks en Korea.
He died alone in a
Rented room — perhaps like in a
Bogart movie.

The end was a cruel hoax.
But his life had been
Remarkable!

    Vato de atolle, el Louie Rodriguez.

1971

FORGIVE?

In the cold compassion
Of my bosom
Habrá perdón
For
My destructors?

To find warmth
In
A
Corazón
Hard-frozen —

When the thaws of
Primaveras have
Come and have gone
    Sería imposible —

Wouldn't one's
Uneasy adversary
    think the same
    heridas that
    expose the heart
    of the heart
    would . . .

Surely welcome
El calor de los
Rayos — rays of
Warmth, however

Sparse?
    Wouldn't he?

Indeed, si el acero
Which pierces deja
Una funda que repela
El calor

    . . . sealing hurts
    forever. Y las
    recompensas se vuelven
    las red-hot scars

That defy the time-healing-time
That fails, and so, and so,
The mind inherits
the burden of
Grotesque
Absurdities
Del pasado.

Thus,
A
Mind is not,
Alas, a sealed-forever heart!

La mente, al contrario,
Is an omniscient,
Indigenous,

1971

Unyielding thing
That
    Knows!

And remembers!

Where does it find
Compassion to forget long
Enough to

Forgive?

PRAWNS FOR A MAYAN PRINCESS

Prawns for a lovely Mayan princess
Bowling alley blues and pay phones
Big Sam is there with his kids.

   STRIKE! How about that?

Bowling night sadness
Family-night. Sunday-eve boredom!
Wet night and exciting apprehensions.
Liquor-store stop half pint
Early times for better times.

There's what's her name and her
Husband — paperback section
Vicarious browsing
sadness
Out of love?
So young!
Yet, love and newness waits out

   The rain

No fish and chips for my
Lovely Mayan princess
Ailing
But tomorrow
Is Monday and
New things begin — for everyone
Mandarin dragons and fish-chopsy-
Suey smells and fortune cookies.
One order of prawns for a lovely
Mayan princess —
   To go, please.

1972

EARLY PIECES

Tony Junior fue el que nos dijo
el hijo de Don Antonio
the ruco who runs the old
beer joint across from the Chino

Que la Rosa the new cantinera the
one who was a wetback
was doing it with all
The chavalitos, just don't tell!

So me and Meño y el culerio carnal de
la coja went over
like we were shining
shoes y no había nadie and she's in
there alone reading a funnybook moving
her lips and she yells,
no hay nadie, ¿más tarde, eh?

And she lifts her dress a little
and we look embarrassed at
each other and she goes back
to the comic and moving her lips.

We stand there todos escamaos and confused
then we run off to Meño's
Garage and when the other vatitos
get there we start bragging how we got
It from the wetback cantinera and Tony
Junior looks surprised so we
All laugh and sit down to jack off.

THIS VALLEY IN SEPTEMBER

Llamas in the month of dying leaves

Summer has left the valley and
Autumn is fleeing.

Next, the freeze and the fog —
valley freeze and valley fog —
looking beyond for a valley spring.

How often have I heard this valley laugh

and moan
and scream in anger

And yield nothing but the four seasons?

1972

"JESSE"

NO TENER Y NO SABER, Jesus Christ!!!

    Chuy cries . . .
    JESUCRIS . . .

To runners with corazón en Hanford
y Mendota y así en otros barrios chinos
eating hot dogs

    WHITE . . .

Nothing whiter, whitier, whitey,
No weed, but wheaties p' almorzar con
filet con huevo —
UN CHINO en un side street of Mexico City
— tu jefito es de la capirucha —
Hablándo español en chino chile piquín

    PEKING!!!!!

Try it on a white hot perro dog.

Not to have and not to know . . .
JESUS CHRISTMINY
Anyhow, ¿con qué me saliste y con qué me
salgo yo?
Out! And forget jess en el valle de lagrimitas
With a capital "L" and Jest let Jess
    HAVE AND KNOW

Wearing a beret patch sobre su Varsity Letter.

Run your heart out boy con brilliantine in
Your greaser hair for scholarships and a hot-
dog
    white.
Coache's glory for your alma momless . . .

BUT JEZ DON'T MARRY MAH DOUDER,
HEAH????

MISA EN FOWLER

Doña Teresa's voice crackled
Like brittle capsules of saliva
and screeched old.

And sister Celeste missed at the organ.

And he laughed aloud and before
He could stop Tony and Chon were
Laughing.

And the father's urgent and severe gaze
Censured them out the door and they
Sat by the curb and drank three-dollar-Joe's
Wine.

And when they started mimicking in
High voices, Doña Teresa's singing,

Ushers ashamed of them were sent to
Quiet them so the mass could continue.

FROM '67 TO '71

Flowers are growing where
we planted bayonets

Hopelessness provides a respite
and reckless impulses subside

I no longer wait for the rains
only cold winter evenings

I wince at revolutionary talk-talk
and a tear and a smile confuse
my prodigies

. . . I don't want to recall
when I became ineffective
but I do

THE HOUR IS TODAY

We look for ways!
No middle road, here.
MIDDLE ROAD!
Only an empty ringing.
REPICANTE CAMPANARIO —
— ¿'onde estás ahora?
"For a glorious while, ése,
we basked in all that noise.
¡Era puro pedo!"
Se llegó la hora
y ahora
me da escame
y gusto.
La alegría of knowing
the waiting is
OVER!
Se llegó la hora
and my finger feathers
the gatillo-strange, awkward
fierrito delicado,
the hour is
TODAY!
 . . . TOMORROW WILL THERE BE
GUNS?
and so, the hour came
out of the imperialistic
necesidades of a savage folkway
slave del tecnico that only
savors violencia in a world
that knows no other climate —
YET, dreams of peace —
LA PAZ, como illusive novia
that would rather not
and knows it hasn't got the
TIME TO BE FICKLE!

VALOR Y LOCURA

Si no fuera
que nos volviámos
insanos
no podriámos seguir

Es insanidad
lo que nos dice
que la lucha es útil

Es locura
la cuál nos hace
desafiar
al monstruo poderoso

No es fé
ni creencias

Solo valor y locura

JACK-OFF HANGOVER

Sunday morning
in church
after Jacking off

The statues looked
like his mother
and his sisters

And he would shut his eyes

And his throat glands wanted
to cry out, NO!

It was not the Virgin Mary
it was Wonder Woman and
Lois Lane —

It was not the Virgin Mary,
it was Maggie Griggs!

— But it didn't matter —

He was unholy, they claimed.

1972

IRISH PRIESTS AND CHICANO SINNERS

He never saw a real priest
They came from Spain or they
Were from Ireland.

    And the growers were fair
    with blond hair — Protestants,
    no doubt!

So when he sinned there
Were Spanish priests and
Irish ones full of bitterness

    And all those sinning Mexicans!

He could never understand, so
He got drunk a lot and went
So bad he was finally sent to
Hell by Spaniards and Irishmen,

And nobody bothered to explain
Any of it to him.

RABIA

I have seen
A rabid dog
Foaming
At the mouth

And I have
Been compelled
To offer up
A dozen Irish rosaries
For a malady
I keep misunderstanding

Because before
The Church
It must have been
Sacred to be
Mad.

1972

ES QUE SE VA MORIR DON CHEMA

Just before the mass
Was their only opportunity.

    And they sang to heaven
    with their eyes shut . . .

ALAVAU SEA EL SANTISIMO
SACRAMENTO DEL ALTAR. . . .

All the viejitos en
Voz alta determined to

    gain absolution for all
    those sweet sins of the past . . .

ME ARREPIENTO, DIOS MIO,
CON UN SUSPIRO Y UNA SONRISA . . .

1972

MORIR DE SUSTO

El bulto no me sorprendió.
Quesque lo 'speraba.
It approached, black from
out of the blackness as the
paranoia me ahogaba

¡'Ama! ¡'Ama! ¡Mamacita!

And alone, curious fear dared
me to look up y vide que'ra
una viejita (¿mi jefa?) que'val
Rosario . . .

    Dios te salve María,
    llena eras . . . llena eras —
    de gracia . . .

1972

SUMMER SOON SUNDAY AFTERNOON

Sitting, waiting,
writing melancholy poetry
about a summer
fast approaching — not daring
to wonder what
will be.

I sip sherry
and warm my belly
and somehow know already
of an impending,
doomsday summer.

(Sherry, hmm, sherry again.
I thought I had forgotten)

Alone, here
I feel
the eerie presence
of priests, pilots,
and poets
and an occasional
dumb-struck farmworker.

(. . . and why do I feel that
in this crowd of lucid
vagueness I am drowning?)

and Romano's line smashes across
my senses — "for I have not been,
I have not been!"

(The sherry is good — the summer
perhaps will be — this Sunday
afternoon is going badly.)

MY MY!

Oh me of mine!!
Life is full
of surprises!

My world! Whose
world?

That's life!
or is it?

Look at where
Willy's at . . .

Surprise, Surprise!

That, indeed is
what life is all
about . . .

That is what makes
life interesting . . .

And Willy is Willy
And Willy's got a
pocket full of
miracles and no
Cliches

LOS CAMPOS DE CORCORAN

Long and lonely, loveless day,
you seem so permanently here now.
But not for very long I pray,
such fixed constancy I disavow.

Long and dry so loveless both
the lonely day and the night
my heart and soul they clothe,
and stretch cobwebs across my sight.

Long and sad the loveless ways
will come and go and come again.
One day bright like the sun's rays
melting wax wings and bringing pain.

Ha! Words!

Empty, putrid cowardly words!
You choke me now as you turn to cotton
when you should stand proud like swords
now don't all of a sudden!

Campesinos!

Your Aztec mother long denied —
gone the days of lavish riches
stepchild now of the Earth — belied
about — slave for other sons-of-bitches . . .
And between a loveless climate

and a mouth that tastes of wool
I am able to deny it —
that it's not the weather — only me, fool.

X — MAS '71

Swirls of PAIN
And dancing
Mayan maidens
At Goyo's y
También en los
Subterraneos de
San Francisco
Rain and prawns
Y una Chinita
Tocándo música
De viento so
Gracefully and
So DEADLY dancing
Seen and heard
In Boston and
Miami — and
Finally back?

Y mis labios
Quedan besándo
La tierra
And I proclaim
que yo olvido sin odio y con
Llanto LLORO.

1972

MONTEREY

Pasó así en una
Noche en la lluvia
De una inesperada tempestad
Que borra la luna escondiéndose
Detrás de Las nubes enloquecidas
Pasó así en aquella playa de
Frenesí y fue la última
Ves que la vide

OH Y OH

The storyteller man's
tale comes in
spinning like flowing silk
entangling and lifting
happy prisoners
on journeys from joy
to sorrow.

Leaping over brooks
of lazy, green frogs
sunning on floating carpets
obviously croaking joylessly
at an idiotic sun
fiercely burning
itself out.

Thinking his
pale — dead
moon — bride
still looks sexy
because of the way
she smirks
so consistently.

And because the teller
is witty or perhaps
the tale well told
all that is related
seems credible.

And the marriage
of the tiny ant
to the giant giant
is not so absurd
after all.

TORRES

Ahijado, Torres, del dulce Nezahualcóyotl
When you were baptized, te elevaron
A la pirámide más alta and from that
Lofty plane atarantozo tu noble
Padrino high priest in attendance
Instilled in you a madness for
Truth y escándalo.

Y con alas de bronce and Quetzal dipped
In blood descendiste
upon us to embrace
Us con tu plumaje de maravilla.

Ahora, tus pinceles, Torres, escupen
On canvas la gloria and the grief
De nuestra Raza.

Sobre tus telas, Torres, relucen las
Manchas de tinta mezcladas with sangre
Transforming into maternal calaveras
Y lechuzas, remembrances
de Hollister
Hills, irragation ditches y cercos
Prohibidos.

En tus telas, Oakland is a black woman
Y la Logan becomes at once un mundo
Moribundo and the hope que ves en tu
Gente.

And we, Torres — " El Queso," pintor del
Barrio — we have mocked your antics,
Tu locura divina, porque nuestras mentes
Torpes no saben comprender the extent
Of your prophetic mind.

S — STREET Y LA CINCO DEL BARRIO

Casi así, así
por las tardes
de la memoria
platiqué con
las palmas
y el jazmín.

Ya no vive aquí
pero fue muy
similar.

Casi así, así,
muy similar.

LA MUERTE DE UN GATO

To rest
    from
Life from
    endless
SOUNDS
    of
Music grown
Cocophonous
And tears
    drowning
The imagery
Like rain
    f
    a
    l
    l
    i
    n
    g
On contact
    lenses
AND, one
So amputated!

There is nothing —
    no more
Scratching itchy
    noses
Fuzzy pussies,
Kitty, kitty.

1972

EL SOL Y LOS DE ABAJO

Darker than most
Lighter than others —
Moreno enough not to have
Made it as an haciendado
Como Don Ramón Hidalgo Salazar.

Descendent soy de los de abajo
arrastrándome voy por la vida
y arrastrado fue mi padre like
his own before — except that
mine compounded the grief by
abandoning his land for another
so foreign and at once so akin
as to be painful.

Y como él I have dragged
Myself and soul in some
Unconscious, instinctive
Search for the splendor
De los templos del sol.

¿Y por dónde me abré
Arrastrado? Does it
Matter? Soy de los de
Abajo — find the gutters
The prisons, the battlefields,
Y los files de algodón —
Ahí me encuentran. En las
vecindades — pronounced
Bah-rrrio now by patronizing

Do-gooders who understand
Us — or rather an image of
Us — decomposed and rearranged
Between eyepiece and lens.

How often have I performed
Inside that ocular tube?
I have squirmed in Logan
Heights and in Barelas.
In the fields of Fresno and
The orchards del condao de
Yuba y con la guardia nacíonal
De Nuevo México en las Filipinas
Y en las cantinas deje mi
Primavera — en la cantina de
La China en Fowler, and the
Boulevard Tavern in Honolulu —
Y en las prisiones también —
De Chino hasta Folsom, de
San Quilmas a la Tuna . . .

Me abré arrastrado
pero los pensamientos
de mi vida los llevo
grabados like the
etchings de Goya and
I remember those times . . .

Times that were tiempos finos —
Chavalitos laughing at Doña

1972

Chole la ruquilla with the ugly
Hump on her back —
La curandera, bruja, life-giving
Jorobada que curó a Don Cheno
Del dolor de ombligo y la
Calentura en la cintura — la que
Daba polvitos for lovers incados
praying to a remarkably reasonable
god that their wives and husbands
wouldn't find out . . .

DIOS TE SALVE REINA Y MADRE
MADRE DE MISERICORDIA
ESTA VELA TE OFREZCO . . .

Virgencita, cause if my husband
Finds out, he will kill me and you
Wouldn't want him in heaven then,
Como asesino, Dios mío . . .

BENDITO SEA DIOS!

Bendito eres sólo cuando concedes
Milagros, otherwise your shrine
Shall be arrumbado y olvidado
Until times of need, death/grief,
Despair y los otros tiempos pasados.

Como raíces de granos enterrados —
Esos son los pensamientos que
Llevo — contradictions and
Paradoxes — that I'm not so
Sure I want to set straight . . .

"Toma, Lupe, lleva este escapulario
que lo bendiga ese cabrón faldillón
del father Kelly and tell him to
keep his hands to himself, ¡que ya
tu 'Apa sabe! Ah, and bring a veladora for
your brother
and the telegram
on the table, don't open it, it may be
from the war saying Toti is dead!"
Muchachos, come and eat!
Después saldrán a jugar.

    IT'S MY TURN TO KICK THE CAN!

Rosa, te quiere mi 'Ama cause
The social worker's here!
¡Dios mío! A visit from the gava!
Alcen la mesa, levanten
Esas garras . . .
Americans were always at my
House. The ones who came to
Strip my Indian flesh from me
And to crucify me with germ-bearing
Labels more infectious than rusty
Nails . . .

    AMERICANS AT MY HOUSE —
Cuando no era el probation officer

1972

Era el councilor de la escuela,
La jura or some long-haired,
Lostlamb, maverick chick offering
Us the world so she could write
Her thesis.

But my dismal world was so
much brighter! My past was
the old barn across the canal
that housed a lechuza that
screeched at night scaring
the children porque era la
ánima de la comadre de mi grama.

    ¡OIGAN!

My abuelita's wrinkled hands
Would clutch a hand-rolled cigarette
And she would squint and lift her
gnarled finger to her ear — ¡oigan!
Es la anima de mi comadre Chonita.

And we would cringe with fear
and would run unashamedly
and hug our jefito's field-
scarred limbs . . .

    . . . ¿Y MI JEFITO?

También arrastrado pero
At least his noble deeds
Are enshrined in ballads . . .

EL CORRIDO DE MI JEFE

A caballo iba el jinete
Se movía por los cerros
Perseguido por los perros
Bien fajado su buen cuete.

Guerillero de la causa
Nobles fueron tus esfuerzos
No por gloria ni por versos
Fuiste a pelear por tu raza.

Y ahora se encuentra tu hijo
en las mismas situaciones
diferentes condiciones . . .

    ¡CHALE!

My actions are not yet worthy
of the ballads . . . me faltan
los huevos de mi jefe and
the ability to throw off
the gava's yugo de confusión . . .

But Chilam Balam's prophetic
Chant has been realized — and the
Dust that darkened the air begins
To clear y se empieza a ver el sol.

    I AM LEARNING TO SEE THE SUN.

A MOCO POME

And if you see
A moco on my
Bigote —

Don't suffer
My shame and
Don't punish
Me with silence . . .

Tell me about it!

1972

SISTERS AND BROTHERS OF CONFUSION

You and I
Saving them
From the police
Should have
Been enough

They were
Only a buncha'f
Drunken Indians
Getting it together
In that Marysville
Bar with knives
On the white side
Of town
And, naturally,
The police
Were called —

. . . So to save
them we said
we knew 'em while
some got clean
away and the other
three we packed
into the van and
took across the
river Yuba
or the Feather
to that city

right across

Y se pelearon otra vez
Anyway and the woman
was getting the worst
Of it

And then the chief
Went after the sister
With the shovel who
Was his ruca's kin —

. . . and the tribal elders
refused to interfere!

So I did what I could
To protect you but
You reminded me you
Were liberated

Yet you kept telling me
All the way back that
What's her name and her
Sister had it coming to 'em

And wise me, and knowing
You, I detected — or did
I imagine it? — a glimmer
In your eye for the

1972

Indio más chief del
Yuba tribe, so I said
Yeah, but, er, ahh . . . and
Very little else

And you reiterated in
Just that fashion that
You were free and glad
You were free and you
Made it quite clear to me
By screaming, "I'm glad
I'm free! Free! Oh, I'm
So glad!!!

If you only loved me
I'd be all those things
plus happy too!"

And I could only blame
Cortez for our retardation
and muttered half heartedly
Something about perhaps
The cycle hadn't come around to
That yet.

VAMOS A DAR LA VUELTA

Otra pa' mi compa Villa

The fastest way I
knew to light
a fire under
my compa's ass
was to say,

"¡Vamos a dar la
vuelta, compadre!"

Y esas vueltecitas
took us to México
in '64 for a
whole summer
in a broken-down
V.W. van that
barely did it.

And once we
went a pata
from Wheatland
to Connecticut
just to get a
six-pack

and when we
returned eight
weeks later,
the party was over

and the sun
was up —
or out —
around!

'61 SUMMER OF LOVE

Do you remember the summer of love
We lived that time
When all was flesh and freedom
And always drinking?

That was the summer we starved
But forgot to
Because there were still
Beautiful things to live for,
Like the Wildside at nine
And pitchers full of beer
With no money.

And at times
Not even for clam chowder
At the Kingfish,
Yet we always managed
From some kind soul
A bowl or two,
And always beer.

(But, Compadre, the clam chowder
Was the essential item
That summer!)

We were millionaires,
Able to afford the finest
And buying it from sun-up to sun-up!
We were rich without a cent,

The four of us and our friends
And always dodging the landlord.
Sleeping warm and late while
He weeded and trimmed the hedge,
Sulking,
And thinking bad thoughts,
Now and again
Cutting a flower for a weed!

(A far more serious sin
Than he imagined us guilty of,
To be sure!)

METAMORPHOSIS — OR GUILTY WITH AN EXPLANATION

I explained
    But they still
    Took almost
    Everything

And the sightless lady
Apologized, but I
Had won!!

I walked out to
The street unescorted
Y me fui por toda
La Efe and it was
Raining hard and I
Began to whistle

    And I was the
    Cucaracha that
    Got away from
    The raid of the
    Black Flag —

Todo catiado, con
Una antena caida
Pero libre and whistling —
My cockroach integrity
Intact!

1972

GABBY TOOK THE 99

Gabby took the 99
The 99 Highway
El Highway 99
EL JAIGUEY
The ninety nine
Donde se requió el troque
Con aquel jentío
The HIGHWAY
Down the 99
Up the 99
Ahi, por todo el 99

El noventa y nueve
As you leave the 99 —

WHO LEAVES???

. . . who ever leaves the
Cold
    ugly
    dry
    hot slippery
    bloody

Dirty
    foggy
    sleek
    powerful
Ninety nine?

NOT RAZA, Okies, Arkies,
Chapos, Armenians — not even
THE MCHIGGENBOTHOMS!

That impersonal 99. And
Not even crosses for the
Dead alongside this road
Of the timeless vanishing
Point.

And in that infinity
You dared to dream, Gabby.

The riches that passed
As you turned trays, loco,
Y el 99 te iba a llevar
Pa ya, Gabby . . .
El Gabby took the 99 —
La salvación!!
. . . and he died in Viet Nam
Of an overdose, ¡pa'
Cabala de chingar!

And Visa laughs
And Dina laughs
And Goshen and Cutler
Y el 99 laughs
And all do the
Tecato tattoo taps.

PORTFOLIO I

The Earth Mother and all her creaturas-with love
La Chicana, su belleza and our fortitude-con cariño y respeto
La Chicana, su fuerza, our belleza-con pride
Chicanos-their 500 years of resistance

MOTHER EARTH

MOTHER EARTH

MOTHER EARTH

LA CHICANA — SU BELLEZA

LA CHICANA — SU BELLEZA

LA CHICANA — SU FUERZA

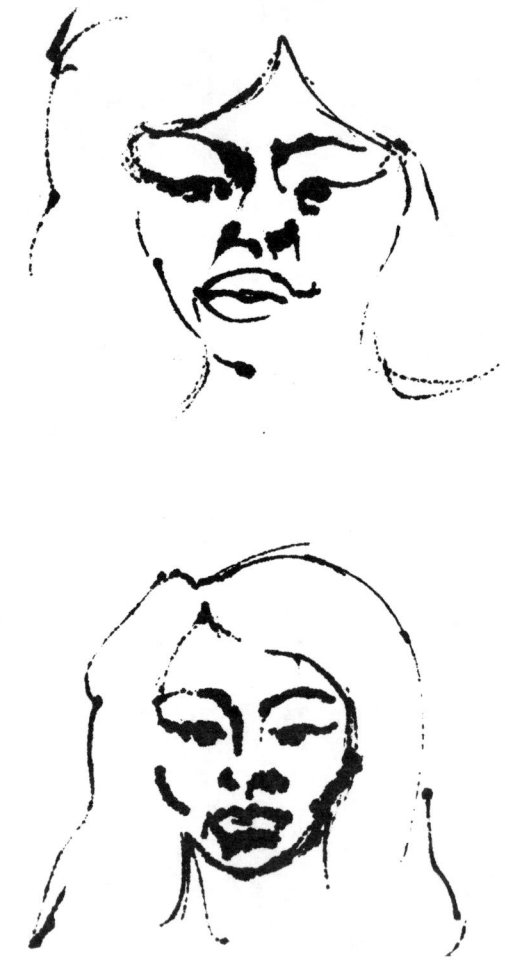

MOTHER EARTH

LA CHICANA — SU FUERZA

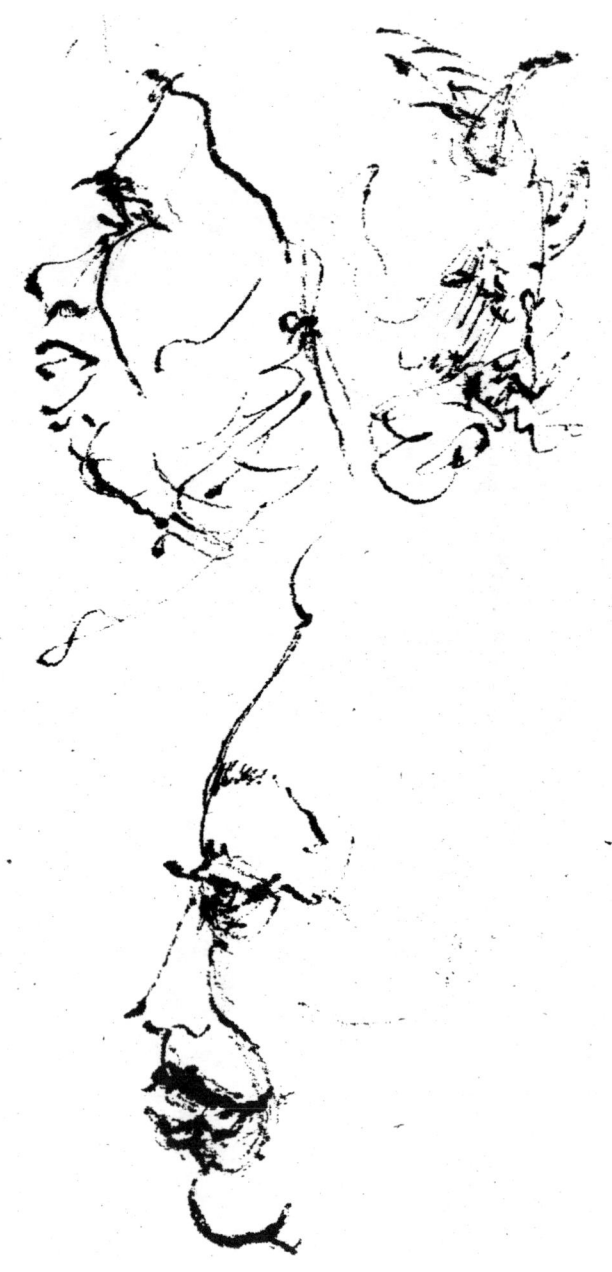

HEIR TO 500 YEARS OF RESISTANCE

HEIR TO 500 YEARS OF RESISTANCE

HEIR TO 500 YEARS OF RESISTANCE

1973

FACES AT THE FIRST FARMWORKERS' CONSTITUTIONAL CONVENTION

Just the other day
In Fresno
In a giant arena
Architectured
To reject the very poor
César Chávez brought
The very poor
Together
In large numbers.

Cuatrocientos delegados
On the convention floor
Alone
And a few
Thousand more
In the galleries —

And outside
(. . . ¡parecía el mercado de Toluca!)

The very poor had come
Together
For protection —

Thousands
From the chaos
Of past, shameful harvests
Culminating

That humble man's
Awesome task
Of organizing
The unorganizables!

Farmworkers!
(Workers of the fields!)

¡Campesinos!
(¡Peones de los campos de labores!)

Not lifeless executives.
Not, stranger yet,
Pompous politicians!

What I saw
Were the familiar
Faces
Of yester grapes
And labor camps.

Body-dragging faces
Baked in the oven
Valle de Coachella
And frost blistered
En las heladas de Sanger
During pruning time.

1973

Faces that have
Dealt with
Exploiters and
Deporters
Y con contratistas
Chuecos.

Faces!

Faces black
From Florida with love
And Coca Cola

Y Raza
De Chicago
Brown Brown
y de Tejas
y Arabes de Lamont
y Filipinos de Delano
y asi gente
That had come
From all the fields
Of all the farmlands
Of America

Farmworkers!
¡Campesinos!
The very poor!

The unorganizables —
Now, at a convention!

Yet,
No fancy, vinyl-covered
Briefcases here,
No Samsonite luggage
Or Botany 500s,

Sólo ropa de trabajo
Pero bien planchadita
Y portafolios sencillos
De cartón
Y cada quién con su
Mochilita
Y taquitos
En el parking lot

Where old acquaintances
Renew friendships
And compare the
Different experiences
Of late

No longer merely
Comparing wages and
Camp conditions like
Before . . .

1973

(. . . ¿a cuánto andan pagando
pa'llá pa' la costa?)

New queries now, reflecting
The different experiences
Of late . . .

(. . . and how many times were
you arrested, brother?)

And the talk of the marketplace
continues
And they listen to
Boastful, seasoned travelers
Who have left, for the time
Being, at least,
The well-worn routes
Of the harvest followers
And they talk of
Strange-sounding places . . .

(. . . pos sabe que yo andaba
en el boicoteo pa'llá pa"
Filadelfia.)

The talk of the marketplace
The parking place
The market lot

The parking lot
Where the families
Were bedded down
For three days
Amidst amistad
Y canciones

Canciones y más canciones
Singing de colores,
About solidaridad
Pa' siempre
And we shall overcome
En español

Singing, singing . . .

Componiéndo corridos
To freeze in time and space
The events
Of that struggle . . .

Año del '73
Presente lo tengo yo
De aquélla infame cosecha
Y el triunfo de nuestra unión

Ay valle de San Joaquín
Campo santo de mi gente

1973

¿Por qué nos tratas tan mal
Como hijos desobedientes?

And they sang of injustice and they sang
Of broken promises . . .

    Los chotas también decían
    Que no querían violencia
    Pero eran puras habladas
    Maltrataban sin conciencia

Y mezclaban los versos de risa y los de valor . . .

    No desafiaba un ranchero
    Un esquiról y su abuela
    Pero nuestro entrenamiento
    Fue en el valle de Coachella

Corridos serios and at times irreverent . . .

    En eso cambió el asunto
    Y empezaron a arrestar
    Echaron corte parejo
    No había pa' dónde arrancar

    Perdóname César Chávez
    Y la Virgen Guadalupe
    Pero antes de que me arresten
    Los voy a hacer que se preocupen

And always they sang of hope . . .

    Ay díganle a mi cuadrilla
    Y a la oficina de Selma
    Que no rompan mi tarjeta
    Que ay les caigo pa' la cena

Even inside
On that floor of decorum
Singing
In defiance
Of Mr. Robert's own rules!

Singing
Singing and joking

    (. . . el que no esté de acuerdo
    con mi moción, ¡que me la apele!)

Ca ca car ca ja das
And table pounding
Belly rolls

Then
Earnestly, without embarrassment
Back to work.
Faces!

1973

Faces de farmworkers —
Organized!
Confident!
Unafraid!

Resoluteness
without impudence —

    (. . . me dispensa hermano director,
    pero mi gente no ha comido.)

Faces!

Faces de campesinos,
Faces of the very poor,
Confident,
Unafraid —

The unorganizables,
The people of the earth —
La gente de la tierra
Today
Very seriously
Contemplating
The ratification
Of Article 37
For history
And forever!

FIERY ROSES

In an old Victorian house
High atop the hills
Above the mission
And the fog

Bathed in the sun-lit
Whiteness of a room
Done up in the tastes of
India, Japan, and
The Zapotecs

We loved amidst
A host of Asian
Peacocks, Olmec jaguars
And fiery, fiery roses.

1973

THE GUARD TOWER AT THE COSUMNES CORRECTIONAL CENTER

You stand impressive
in your stoical awesomeness

Surveying a sorry sight
of desolation hollowed
many times over by
scores of martyred Raza,
political Blacks, and your
own addicted children and
their derelict fathers.

Over all that misery, innocuous
for the moment, you stand defiant —
sterile erection, symbol
of America.

Ironically, to the right, the
flag flutters, anxious to
heave accolades in your
direction — the touch of
thirteen swords knighting
your futile efforts, no
longer illuminated by
fifty darkened stars.

Up-tight, upright, and powerful
tower of power — yet this
humble poet dares to
nullify your lofty grandeur,
stripping your cover as bare
as the damaged denizens
your powerful binoculars
denude with every methodical scan.

Bring it up close, tower,
take a good look!

1973

THE FORM OF A KISS

What is the form of a kiss?
Indefinable, yet so distinct
on recall.

There is shape and volume,
there is dimension to a kiss.

All influenced naturally,
by what is being kissed.

A mouth, say, responds unlike
a breast — even a nipple to a nipple,
(Some require suction; others
become delicious obstacles
for a furtive tongue.)

And a closed eye that slowly
opens to that moistured touch
introduces a fluttering that
is different than the lobe-
softness of a permissive ear.

The nape of the neck is not
as impersonal as the
forehead or the tip of an
up-turned nose. (But just
beneath the nostrils, right above
the upper lip, ahhh!)

And that hollow, soft, sweet
hollow, near the shoulder,
becomes alive as muscles twitch —

And of course, the form of
a navel kiss depends ultimately
on the handywork of some
midwife or obstetrician
long ago.

And so the clit!
So exhilaratingly more
delightful, that form
than any other . . .

The form of a kiss. The
Myriad, mystical
variations of the
form of a kiss!

LA GINA

September 23, 1973
They're playing "Volver, Volver"

On your birthday
    mi hija —
    that important one
    of
18 years in a cruel
World that you have
Made less cruel.

    De mi sacáste
A penchant for the ideal
And the romantic.
    De tu dulce y
    bella mamá
    sacaste todo lo
Que es bueno and lasting —
I don't take credit for
That unique occurrence.

    But providence saw fit to
    bestow upon you those two
    wonderful and necessary contradictions—
Ideals, as well as romantic
Notions tarnish —
Expect it!!!
But goodness is the countering

Balance,
    You have both!
    Te felicito,
    hijita —
Tu papá de las cantinas
Y los callejones
De oro.

1973

PACHECO PASS

There's a huge, blue lake
At the base of Pacheco Pass
A man-made-for-growers-by
Agribusiness-unnatural lake

A blue-green gem amidst the
Arid foothills to boost Reagan
And a multi-million dollar
Industry to better and bigger
Things and hot summer fun.

Lake of blue blood — y el sudór
De campesinos who
In the same hot summers are
Being beaten
By hired goons in the
Fertile valleys of despair,

Pacheco pass,
Ancient bridge-gap de mi
Gente — awesome gateway
To yet another valle salado,
Now a scenic drive — with
A four-lane, super highway
And a view of that lake,
Superficial mantle, unable
To cover up la sangre de
La Raza que todavia mancha

El camino viejo — vereda peligrosa
De los pobres — hoy retumban los
Gritos del pasado, barely audible
Above the roar of high-powered
Evinrudes —

¡Se acabó el jale, Raza!
¡Ya estufas con la uva, vámonos!
¡Allá nos vemos en Hollister!
¡Nos guardan una carpa!
¡Cuídense por ahí en el Pacheco Pass!
¡Y antes de empezar el viaje
Las comadres se echaban
La bendición!

Pero cuánto troque con mucho
Cuidado — con rezos and baling
Wire y familias enteras left
Their dreams at the bottom
Of that lake?

And today there is this lake
For the insensitive, white man
Who has wisely shifted the violent
Carnage far from this, his paradise
Retreat, to Lamont and Coachella.

And the beating of women and children

1973

In Fresno and Lodi is far removed
From this lake at the base of
Pacheco Pass!

1973

BARRIO LANDMARK

The Alkali Club
Opens at six in the
Morning and more than
Once from an all-night
Bout with love, wine
Or intellect, I have
Found myself there
At the pallid hour
One with the straggling
Dead on that corner
Of desolation
At 10th and E

And with them I have
Re-lived unrequited
Dreams and I have
Envisioned new ones
Of grandeur

And more times than not
I have felt at once
Alien and one with them

And once I even
Realized my own
Hypocrisy after
Having been kissed
By a wino who

Bought me a drink
Because his memory is
Better than mine — since
I used to consider
Them all strangers —

    " . . . this one's on me, poet,
      for that time long ago."

And there for a flashing
Eternity my very own
Loneliness was
Vanished

1973

THE MELANCHOLIA OF BEING A POET AT CHRISTMAS TIME

Sitting on a bench
At a shopping center mall
Decked with boughs of
Plastic holly

Drinking coffee, safe
And warming from the
Cold outside

Watching yuletide shoppers
Impressed with the
Marketplace atmosphere
Devoid of natural smells
And energies — more like
A surreal carnival of
Harried, hurried blurs
All chiming tinga-lingly
To the bells of canned
Music chasing imaginary
Reindeer

And I'm filled with
A peculiar sadness
That reminds me
That I've always
Cried more around
This time of the year
Since the time I was

Very young

And it hasn't always
Been of happiness

LATE AUTUMN

In my backyard
The ivy and the
Elm trees
Have become
A veritable
Forest fire.

And drinking
Hot coffee there
In the brisk dusk
Feels good.

Before long
A coat will be
Necessary.

And every day
The fire plunges
Earthward.

AT FORTY, HUEVOS AND PRIDE CAN LEAVE YOU DEAD

The streets were screaming
"They looking to dust you, ése,
cause you fucking with' a chick
of that young vato and his dudes
don't dig veteranos anyway!"

— ¡Ponte trucha, ese! —

So, let 'em kill me, ¡pinches
mocosos!

And the streets screamed aloud.

And they did kill him — and he
was the wrong guy.

And he could've told 'em all
along, but that thing of honor
was involved and the streets
wept in silence and pride strutted
alongside the coffin.

PURPLE MOON OVER PORTLAND TOWN

Each day of sorrow
I consider my
association to that
purple moon

moving across
the infinite concave
taking forever
your dreams of me

and I choke
in the thin air
of cold minuscule
crystals that
slash at my
lidless eyes

crying crimson tears
for our beautiful
and grotesque madness,
yours and mine.

1973

LA REINA MANCORNADORA

Cuando bajé del cielo
Reina, reina majestosa
Te víde

Y no pude imaginarme
Lo que sería ser tuyo

En eso me extendiste
Tus brazos
Y me ofreciste tu
Hermosura blanca
Con una sonrisa
Seductiva

Y tus labios se partieron
Y llegué loco
A tus pies —
Lleno de esperanzas

Y allí me encontró al
Tapón rabón
Para decirme
Que me las cortara —
Que ya eras de'l — y lloré'
Y tú te escondiste en las nubes
Y jamás te volví
A ver

¡Te rayaste, taponcito! ¿Cómo le vas hacer?
¡Esta vez te fuiste
Grande!

1973

SE FUE RICARDO

Quería ser mi carnalito
y cuando le dije que no
— que ya era hombre —
se ha de haber sentido

Y yo
que quería hacerlo
sentirse seguro
le quité la seguridad
del carnal calote — el que
todavía le
hacia falta

Y solo
no pudo con el gusano
ni yo con su cruz
— y se fue —
dicen que
hacia rumbo al sur

1974

FIVE, ALONE

Five Chicanos
On the nine o'clock
Special
To Veracruz
All together
Each alone

Camacho dreams
Of cool beaches
Y cocteles de
Ceviches

And Rita cradles
Robert's pale green
Death mask, reminder
Of last night's sour pulque

And Xavier complains
The train stops
Too much as he
Drinks Robert's
Brandy

And I sip a
Warm Corona
And eat a
Spicy torta
And I am reminded

I forgot to bring
Along some
Toilet paper

Bitch!
Bitch!
Bitch!

And we are not tourists
We almost convince ourselves
But the spirit hovers
It is there

And the conspiracy
We suspect continues
As the porter comes
Along warning of a
Hurricane weekend

The spirit hovers
We settle back
And we pass
Colonias cloaked
In nightness and
Nightmares of
Incredible
Poverty

1974

And we try not
To see the distance
Lit up with neon signs
For Firestone and
Of course Coca Cola

And the now dry
Ancient/modern
Lago de Texcoco
Falls behind
As we head for
The mountains of
Orizaba and Córdova
High, high, and higher

Trying to forget
The neon malady
(Searching for roots
Is so unclear!)

So we decide
To get drunk
With beer and
Brandy boiler-makers

And the lonesome whistle
From the engine
Snaking up ahead

Lends the night trip
An air of adventure
And the nostalgic
Fantasies produce
A dizziness that's
Almost as pleasant
As it is false and
We brace to pretend —
And we move toward the
Coast feeling weighted
Down

If only we didn't know
So much — five Chicanos
On the nine o'clock
Special to Veracruz

    All together,
    Each alone!

1974

LAY-OVER IN MAZATLAN — ONE YEAR TO THE DAY

In slow motion,
At times suspended
In the heavy heat
    the seagulls soar
    cocky and indifferent,
    high above the
    terminal

And in that blinding
Suffocation, I suffer
In the memories of
A sun-selling
Postcard you sent
Me — a year ago to
The day
    saying how
    you missed
    me and how
    you loved me

And today, I write
    a poem

Waiting for transportes
Norte de Sonora
To take me back
To that engaño
That dissolved

    our magic
    forever

Y sigo viajando
En camiones de segunda
    that carry me
    closer to that
    other heat sin
    aire acondicionado

My thoughts wrapped with
Ribbons del color
De la traición

EL TANDITO DEL ANGELO

When you
Walked in
Se le cayó
La mollera
A la calavera

Y no quedó
Nada más
Que tu
Tandito
De vato loco
Veterano

And the barrio
Crowned you
Forever
Prime-prince
Angel
Character

1974

ALWAYS DO AS YOU ARE TOLD THE BEST WAY YOU KNOW HOW.

The bailiff gave me
One of those
You're-on-my-turf-now-punk
Looks and exhorted me to
Call the judge YOUR HONOR

So I said, "fuck you very much"

What?

I said, "thank you very much,
Your honor!"

Oh, I see. That's better.

"Uh Hum,"
Dije yo. . . .

1974

THE MOVEMENT HAS GONE FOR ITS PH.D OVER AT THE UNIVERSITY, OR THE GANG WARS ARE BACK

What has happened to the Movement, camarada?
What has happened to la causa and the guns?

All those vatos de proposals y programas
Federales, ¿Dónde están?

Qué paso con EOP and education
weren't we going to build a nation
called Aztlan?

What became of the berets and revolution
y las marchas and all that yelling
¿De qué sirvió?

Where do you suppose they've gone,
all those bad-ass bigotones
que llegaron shouting RAZA
y viva EL BARRIO
and they couldn't even roll their R's?

And what happened to political awareness?
All those programs that we started
in the barrio —
taken over by those nice republicanos —
los que hacían malas caras
when we used the word Chicano!

And all those plants and agents — all the
ones that
infiltrated — ¿Como no los conocimos?
Like the dude that kept my jefa
from that meeting 'cause security
was tight? Right! He turned out to be
a cop!

What has happened to the movement, camarada?

Well, compadre, if we use reason
we should seriously applaud all
the efforts of our mission and our vision
as we see how much our lot has
been improved. And those cosas
que eran malas that that federal
commission has removed.

Por ejemplo
Ya la tienda fea de Don Pedro is no
longer — Y el jardín de Doña
Julia ya no está —

Now that high rise in the barrio — and
the Safeway on the corner — they
could surely be the pride of our
fair city

But we'll need a new proposal to repaint

1974

all that graffiti — ¡Ay! Qué Raza
no se aguanta — just what
do these people want?

If they'd only go to college so that they
could learn Marxism
and learn of the benefits of cultural
pluralism!

Now consider los colegios and the
progress de los estudios Chicanos
donde MEChA mano a mano
has just won the intramural cup!

Y los profes y estudiantes siguen
siempre deligentemente pa' delante
all keep searching for those stipends
in the sky.

Y los de las corbatitas con sus jales
de directors ya empezaron
a new barrio por allá por Washington
con Don Nixon de vecino
where the cherry blossoms bloom
far away from all this gloom.

¡¡Pos mire usted, pero no!
¡Qué barbaridad!

Meanwhile, to the South a
gentle wind begins to blow.
Ojala y tenga paciencia
ese viento de Bolivia.
Y los guerillas de Chiapas
de Guerrero y Guatemala
tengan fe en nuestra conciencia
ya nos trae la confusión —
pero de allí , han de salir
los frutos de nuestra potencia.

1974

DON'T EVER LOSE YOUR DRIVER'S LICENSE

Greyhound riding lonesome blues
not to mention the turmoil and despair
of the terminals — pimps and pushers
and frightened grandmas —
refugees from Middle America
and sadistic cops.

And you ride side-by-side
old people going on their last journeys
and young people on their way
to new adventures and dreams
leaving their burdens to the mountain
and eventually
vice versa

And the dreams seem nearer
as huge, smiling billboards
Proclaim a grand America
Out there — somewhere — as the
Gloom rolls on, along
Futuristic freeways —
Modern long knives —
Slicers of old barrios

And finally having left the driving
To insulting drivers
A static voice
Crackles a thank you for

Going Greyhound and
You feel grateful
In a hateful sort of way

Knowing you've been taken
For a ride — side-by-side
Old people going on their
Final journeys.

UNA LAGRIMA POR TU AMOR

She turned slowly, and said,
"Estoy aquí pistiando — ¡Porque
me gusta! — What did you expect,
a sad story?"

Pos I'm sorry!

He turned slowly, and said,
"Estoy aquí pistiando — ¡Porque
me gusta! — What did you expect,
a sad story?"

Pos I'm sorry!

1974

ORITO DEL BARRIO CON SAFOS

For Tomás Atencio,
The patient listener

Me decía Don Alber Diaz
Sentao en la resolana,
"A la plebe de hoy en día
No se le puede decir nada."
Sí, ¡fijese, quesque no quieren entender¡

And across the street
On the wall del cleaners
De la Terry por la trece
Un chavo had
Spray-canned
His anguish
In eleborate
Simplicity —
"Geneva, my baby,
Geneva, my love,
Por vida."
. . . knowing that cat was hurting!

I looked at Don Alber — ancient Tarascan
Sage, y le dije,
"Cuénteme otra vez
De Don Lázaro Cárdenas
Pa' que así no me vea llorar."

1974

THE PEOPLE'S REPRESENTATIVE

A song to people afraid of success.   Vaginal diagram

With our hearts
And our faces
We worked
Our collective
Brown ass
To get you there

And in gratitude
You grasped your
Handful of
Yellow daffodils
In an impressive
Clenched-fist
Salute

And as the flowers
Wilted you ran your thumb
Between your toes
And rolled the dirt
Like coils of greasy
Black clay into
Tiny spirals

And before too long
You began studying
Another white

1974

EL BARRIO EN ENERO

En las tardes invernales
Al obscurecerse
Las calles de mi barrio
Se transforman con
Los juegos de niños
Olores de cenas
Y los alaridos de
Madres anciosas

Todo se empieza
A integrar con
La niebla azul
De las humaderas
Sobre un cielo
Enegrecido

Y nadie le teme
Al frío de enero
Las niñas en blanco
Corren al catecismo
Y los muchachos
Se fijan sin disimular
Y siguen jugando

Y los perros se 'olen
Y se desengañan
Y siguen en busca
De algo

Y por allá se oye
El chillido
De una sirena
Y un destino
Inevitablemente
Se apreviene.

TRES CANTOS EN VANO

Le canto al Roger
ex-beret
Rock drummer
dreamer
street
and family man
(. . . the quiet one of
all the brothers,
mystics all, music
forever!)
Le canto al Roger
dead at 26

Le canto al Danny
búfalo-big
and Brown
and bad
shot for trying
to hustle
a Black brother
pimp who
should have
remembered that
Danny kicked ass
and went
to jail
when Sac high
blew out in '69

(. . . Blacks and Browns
against the world — all
carrying "Free Danny"
picket signs at the
district office till
the demands were
"negotiated.")
Big, bad Danny, I sing to you
dead at 22

Le canto al Tony
a él,
who used
to laugh
at death
and say
that someone
said death's
got to be
the finest
high

Cause
you only
do it once!
(. . . and he assailed Indian
mystics and the Jesus freaks
for answers he needed but

1974

never accepted.)
Le canto al Tony de Visa
dead at 24

Tres carnales dead in vain
tres cantos en vano
how many more lamentable
dirges must we wail out
to be carried by the wind?

Must we continue to wring
our hearts como estropajos?
Do we merely walk away from
wasteful gravesites and learn
to suffer in our own solitary
way after each fresh burial?

(Canto en vano, pero
canto para poder
aguantar).

ARROZ IS ARROZ IS ARROZ

Sons and daughters
Of so many
Yaquis

Lindas
Muñecas shatter

As federal
Money echoes
In the eyes
And ears
Of maniacos
Running amuck

And the streets
Del barrio
No cambian — they
Are life and
Death — much
As before

And we dare to be amazed
By these false failures
Which just may be our
Salvation!

SE PUEDE?
Simón que ¡sí se puede!

Some day!
On our own terms, ese!

Fíjate que yo
Dejé mi carrucha
Unlocked for
A whole day or two
In Gardenland
And nothing was taken!

¡Pos no tienes nada, guey!

Precisely my sentiments
To you sir, and for
The world!

We will be driven mad
Until insanity
Makes sense to us!
So, smiling, I went
With Charlie to borrow
Money from bigotes
At the El Paso, and
Before I could order
I had bought a velíz
And a flashlight
That didn't flash

1974

Y las bisagras
Del velís fell off
But for two bucks
It was cheap
Y la lana fue prestada,
Anyway
And we even got a swig
Del mismo wine and
Chepa felt so badly
She cooked me free
My favorite dish

And I recalled
How years before
Doña Trini with
The tattooed crosses
On her arms
Used to cook a mean
Esteque pica'o
A la chicana
Using round steak
Entonces, porque
No había inflation

And last night
Chepa, who was taught
By Doña Trini
Guizó también an

Excellent chicana
But this time
With stewing meat
Porque así le enseñó
Su mamá
To deal with hard times
And to prepare us all
For el día de la Raza

¡Sí se puede!,
Someday soon
On our terms
If we
Want it!

And that day
Will be
My Raza's day,
And it can be
Today
And everyday
Porque mi raza
No se raja
Cause oppression
Keeps us razor sharp
And we realize — and
We're glad no one
else does — that our

1974

Salvation is our
Own desmadre
And vice versa.

And when we harness chisme, we'll have
Mother nature
and the derelict dog
On our side
Y tantitos beans
Con arroz y salsa
Picante will always
Be steak to us just
Like before.

Simón que ¡sí se puede!
Someday
On our terms,
Ese!

My jefitos
Were stone fatalists, carnal,
And they did fine —
Ask my brothers
And my sisters.

My Jefa's válgame dioses
And my jefe's
Ay-que-vida-tan-desgraciádases

Took us safely for years
Up that rippling
Migrant stream
Alongside fishes
Who smiled at us cause
We carried no hooks
To rip apart
Their gaping mouths

Simón que, ¡Sí se puede!
Someday when they, and
Even we, least suspect it,
But on our terms, ése —
On our time —
On our day of our people —
On our DIA DE LA RAZA!

1974

A HAPPY DOG IS

Where is
That dog
That just
Turned
The corner
Smiling
Coming
From?

THE FACELESS WONDER

Mando,
I Never
knew you
had
fat
cheeks

Then,
you shaved
your
beard

And not
even
Manuela
loved you!

THE GRAIN SHED

In one of my childhood Februaries
I recall sitting warm with my dog
on the sunshine side of the old
grain shed, warm, bright, and safe.

While my dog dozed scared, I listened
to the force of the cold, tin-roof ripping,
out-house-door slapping, hinge-flapping
wind come whipping

Round the side passing us safely by
carrying sage brush and milk buckets,
a rooster fluttering, and other debris,
and I'd feel warm, safe, good!

I'd feel good like it has been hard
to feel that good in the Februaries
of my now of gentler winds and the old
grain shed, solid, safe is plainly gone forever.

HOTEL ROYALTY

Bello puerto de Veracruz
I saw you
once before
long ago
at carnival —
time
with Carlos
and Carrillo
y una gabachita
de flores

Now, a second time around
with Tafoya and Camacho
staying at the inn of
ancient mariners
I appreciate
you more

Perhaps because we're so broke
and we can only afford this
second-story room by the sea —
a huge room,
reeling and peeling
with rusty
hammock rings
paint stuck
to the wall
and one enormous

double-window door
que sale al balcón

So that from every part
of the room we're able to
see the girls sitting on
the sea wall below — even
from the open shower/toilet
stall combination kept in
constant service — the shower
for cooling off, the other
for strengthening frayed
pucker strings.

We drink Tecates and shell
camarones
and watch the block of
ice melt in the sink right
before our eyes and we
    light up and
    get high
    tripiándonos con un
    plunger on the
    ceiling making
    vortex ringlets
    and we smoke green
    cigars to dispel
    the paranoia

1975

    and take turns
    standing under
    the shower and
    sitting beneath the
    high ceiling's lazy
    fan

We laugh and we joke and sing
and the maids giggle and bring
their friends to see the locos —
and for that they
forgive us our trespasses and
our inability to tip lavishly
    for living so
    lavishly and
    before too long
    the maids fight
    the bell boys
    to see who will
    bring us ice and
    limes — all for
    free now, just
    for the chance to
    be part of that
    locura

Y ya tarde nos vamos a los
Portales a comer mariscos
Y a pistiar rones y a escuchar
El ritmo jarocho and finally
By the light of the dawn and
To the sounds of bell and horn
Boueys in the bay we sing our
Winding, cobbledSTONED way
Toward the sea once more to
Sleep soundly con el murmullo
De las olas and a cool welcomed
Sea breeze that is finally
Released by the calm sea at
Dawn

    Bello puerto
    de Veracruz
    hasta que nos
    conocimos

1975

EL PADRE NUESTRO AND THE PARK

Pa' Juanishi

I walked
The silver-bladed park
This primrose morn
And the remoteness
Obscured all cityness
And I praised
Something or other
In reverence of —
Some sort — probably
Of the park itself —

> A park I have
> Neglected because
> I always thought
> The country meant
> Out of town.

And here it's been,
This park — so near
My house — casi kitty-corner,

> Como quien dice —
> This simple, yet
> Majestic park!

But it was the sun!

¡Fue el sol!
That made me notice
Porque, alas! — a las
Seis y media de
La baraña
On a cold December,
Morning,
I witnessed that sun
Ahí en el parque
Engaged in a battle
For dominion with
The fog!

And to my amazement
The sun dispatched post haste
The fog toward the
Two rivers and to
The bottom lands
Having become,
It seemed to me,
Fed up with having
To put up with bothersome
Crap like that — ¡El Sol Enojado!
And he instructed
The rays to prick
And shaft the few
Remaining leaves

1975

    And directed
    them to more or less
    take command over
    the whole day — pero
    con respeto
Instructing them to
Be discreet and stay
Out of the way
Of the park elders —
Como los troncos
Toscos de los Encinos,
The elms and the redwoods
And of course, to watch
Out for squirrels and
The flower beds

. . . the Sun's rays —
Barely getting used
To the day's chores
So early in the morning
Wondered why he was
So wise

    . . . and proceeded to
    transform that
    silver morn to
    golden wonderment

1975

THE BARRIO ARTIST/TEACHER

Pa'los del RCAF

Because to create
Is to give life
The barrio artist/teacher
Commits acts of love . . .
And risks
Seeming selfish.

But

To look into
the eyes
Of a child
Discovering
The magic
Of color
Amidst squalor —

To see
A stone
Vato loco
Caressing
A ball of clay —

To discern
As wrinkled
Fingers forget

The pain of aging —

It has to be a
Selfless
Selfishness.

1975

UNTIL THEY LEAVE US A LOAN

> . . . *as related to me by*
> *Elías, alias, Eelye.*

Back then, José, we knew
McKinley Park as Clunie Pool.
Fancy, ese, with a high-board
y todo el pedo — and strictly
for gavas!

Pero después que'l county
sent the sheriffs to
halt our brown nakedness
at both rivers — quesque we
was causing wrecks near the
new bridge! — pos quién
les manda a los mensos!
Serves 'em right for running
freeways right above our
swimming holes — ¿Te curas?

So we all cut off our
patched-up-marble-knees pecheras
and we invaded Clunie Pool
and routed the gavas
and for three beautiful days
the barrio owned Clunie, ese!

And not even a lifeguard around
— the last one sent down from
parks and recreation cuitió
without reporting nothing,
¿Qué tal?

And we swam and we peed
in the water for three days
and three nights — parecía
una factory de chocolate,
¡por Dios santito! — a bronze
smelter, ése, in the heat
of July and a glistening,
blue-silver fish hatchery in
the moonlight, are you on
to that one?

Pero ya sabes, carnal,
the solid, stolid neighbors
who were used to the
solemn, cemetery stillness
of that beautiful park
de volada le hablaron a la ley
— but they came too late, ése,
the park was ours!
Public park, ¿Qué no?

Y de ahí pa'cá it became our
classroom, ése, a sex education

1975

forum for young dudes — ¡maniácos!
and the Rose Garden right
there, carnal, in front of
the police academy was the
place a lot of vatos lost
their maiden-heads and began
to wonder why white chicks
fucked and ours went to
catechism, except for Connie
and Lupe's sister, la mayor,
who later turned out way, way
ahead of all the others in
every respect, know what I
mean, ése?

Y luego después, que curada,
watcha — we used to ride around
the park en Mercs y Chevies,
¿Tú sabes? — And C°2 pistols
in the back seat — just circling
the pinche park, como guardias,
Dig? Drinking Ripple, white
and red, and for the rucas,
Pagan Pink.

And today — pos' ya sabes, you've
seen it on Sundays, ése!
O' Simón, and the annual menudo
bowl — ¿y quién empezó los
Barrio Olympics?

You heard about Villa taking
first place for bogarding las' year?
¿Qué pulmones del indio, verdad?

Y cuando la Jenny y el Sam have
a family reunion — ¡ya estufas!
and then there was the fundraiser
for little Joey — ¿te acuerdas?
Man, that was heavy!

Sheet! ¿Sabes qué, ese? 'Cept
for a few fights, tú sabes, ¿al
punto pedo? — Like when Billy
the boy got knifed, man, we've
done all right by McKinley!

¿Sabes lo que me cai más de aquéllas?
I don't know if you've picked up
on it, ése, ¡pero casi ya no quedan
muchos gavas! They're moving out,
have you noticed that? It's hard
to tell; I don't know if you've
even noticed!

But you know what else, ese?

1975

I heard a new freeway's gonna
come through here — did you
hear anything?

Qué quemada, ¿Verdad?

But I've been looking at this
big park over in Carmichael

No, ¿pero tú sabes?

¡Chale, ése! No la chinguez. . .
I was just thinking, man!

¿Qué dicen haya en la universidad? —
Plan your future,
Tú sabes.

YOU KNOW I WOULDN'T IF ONLY I COULD MASTURBATE

But it isn't as if I didn't
pay attention, merely that
I would rather not as though
not even care!

Yet, last night we lost a battle.

And we drank until we got drunk
and celebrated
worse than if
we had won!

And we made love!
And we made love!
And we made love!

We made love,
several times!

1976

EL VETERANO

*. . . Pa'l Angelo Alvarez at
his gravesite, a true street
warrior and friend . . . guárdame
un trago, ¡ay te llevo!*

After that age
When you've
Been around
There will always
Be confrontations
With power-challenging
Upstarts

And that is as
It should be

And you stay on top
For as long as you can
Hoping the inevitable
Fall will be graceful
And executed with class

And you can deal
With all of that —
Even bask in the
Confidence
Of your wisdom, and
In the knowledge

That you can still
Take 'em all on!

And you are
Careful to maintain
Respect for the
All-knowing veteranos,
Como el Esteban y el Sam . . .

But things being
As they should be
Sooner or later
You have to go
Up against a young
Warrior you trained
Yourself — and the
Test alters your
Style

And more than likely
You'll come through it
Unscathed and wiser —
Until you run up
Against two of them!

Then you go down
Knowing you didn't
Teach those two

1976

Any class at all

It is as it should be

And then there's the
Few that go all the
Way — all the way

Como tú, carnal

All is as it should be.
The balance —
The rhythm —
The eternal cycle. . . .

1976

... A poem with the title at the end.

What is my lovely lady's
Preference on this warm
Bright morn of firm,
Light-bathed thighs on
The aftermath of
The sun's explosion?

Is it a time to bask
In that warmness awhile
Then proceed —
Naughty but nice?

Or shall we complement
The fast moving morning
Light with a fast
And furious bout?

Or shall we be audacious
And compete with the
Radiant, ravaging
Energy of the white
Light and brace/embrace
Ourselves for
Down and dirty?

How, Baby?
How shall we argue today?

LOVE/HATE

1976

FALTAN QUINCE PA' LAS CUATRO

Cuarto Esquinas
tiene sin fin
el mundo

Cuartro rincones
finales tiene
mi cuarto

Faltan quience pa' l invierno

Y yo despaché
llorando
a dos hojas
rojas

Con las lluvias
se caerán otras

Las escarchas
helarán las
que quedan

1976

TWO LETTERS

One day
I shall write
to each
a letter
explaining how
my own plight
is a blight
because they,
each in
her own way,
have made
in my life
the most
profound
upheavals
of my years
to date

And those
two letters
will become
historic and
scholars of
aplomb
and of very
astute insights
will try
to make much

of such an
important
episode and
miss the
whole point

Only we three
will ever know
who walked
away from this
damaged the
least of all

1976

THEY SENT MEN TO MATCH MOUNTAINS

A Washoe brave
returning from
the hunt befell
a strange and
frightful scene
in the snow high
above the
frozen lake so
awesome he cried
like nothing
had moved him
thus before

Y corrió
sobre la niéve
a avisarle
a su abuelo

Yet, an
indescribable
fear kept
him from approaching
the wise old man
because it was
a fear somehow
enmeshed in shame

But the old one
eased the warrior's
task so he could
relate his tale
of horror — of having
seen men eating
each other and
freezing in the
snows of the upper pass

El viejo no se conmovió
and before the young man
could repeat the scene
in another fashion — in
a way it could be
believed

The old one
touched the young
man's eyes and said
you have witnessed
the strangers who
have come to
take our mountains

And you have seen
the grimness of
times to come — the
blood on their bared

1976

teeth against the
whiteness of the
snows is a sign of
their unyielding
determination to
take our mountains
and our plains and
our rivers.

Why? Asked the
young man. Why?

Without changing
his countenance,
the old man replied,
because they have
no mountains
of their own.

LA YARDA DE LA ESCUELITA

La escuelita al pie del monte
Es chica, así es que
Los niños vienen en varios tamaños,
Unos pequeños y ya en el libro ocho
Otros altos, galgos
Y apenas en el tercero.

Alrededor de la maestra
Acurrucados de miedo — como pollitos —
Se amontonan los del baby room
Asustados desde septiembre,
Y así permanecerán hasta junio
Cuando pasen al libro primero.

La escuelita al pie del monte
Porque está en las sierras
Que dan tan poco
Los niños se visten p'al frío
No pa' verse bien
Y el ropaje corre desde
Botas mucho muy grandes
Y túnicos hechos a mano
Que han venido pasando
Desde cuando de hermana a hermana —
Así que las medidas
Son de por ahí del medio

Y la mestra

Estólido monumento de seguridad —
Cambia su compostura
Mil veces al día-pa' cada mal
Un genio negro, pa' cada bien,
Una sonrisa y un aprecio.

Y cuando no está segura
Lo esconde biend — como cuando
Pasó lo de Rosendo — acongojado
Rosendo, con las cejas fruncidas
De miedo — esperando lo peor
Por haber dejado la pelota
Salirse del cerco — Ay, po'recito
Mu' chito — !y él que nunca
Se mete en males! Por que
No podriá ser uno
De aquellos otros canallas
El que dejó salir esa maldita pelota?

Así es que ahora la mestra
Se encuentra incierta
Y los niños que se prenden
De la cintura
Ni cuenta se dan
Y ya para entonces
Los traviesos le llaman
La atención
Porque por allí por los escusados

1976

Cerca de los pinavetes
Les andan bajando los bloomes
A unas mu'chitas que pretenden
¡Escándalo!

    "Boys! Boys!"

Y en lo que la mestra trata
Con ese cuento de nunca acabar
Rosendo brinca el cerco
Sobre la bola — ¡no me vido! ¡no me vido!

Y entre regañadas, la Miss Chávez
Da gracias a Dios y chequea
Su pulsera y el chico
Del libro seis que ha andado
Brincando con anticipación
Porque él es el que suena la campana
Y ha estado esperando
Con mil ansias esa
Momentosa ocasión desde que
Se empezó el reses
Ahora al fin, recibe sus órdenes —
¡La campana!

Y al instante lo domina
Un ataque espasmoso
Y con las dos manos

¡Suena y brinca
Brinca y suena!

Y el sonido repicante suelta
Una implosión que ahoga
El budicio
Y de todas partes de la yarda
Convergen los niños a matacaballo
Riendo y gritando
Gritando y unos llorando
Tropezandose y puchando,
Acabando con todo.

Unos traen flores
Y puños de piñon
Y otros el bate y la pelota

Y los más grandes, con calma
Apagan bachas de Golden Grain
Y escupen ploga — los más
Verdes con caras verdes
Y los otros carcajeándo.

Y en la liña la mestra
Organiza sus columnas

    Boys there!
    Girls here!

1976

Tony, get rid of that frog!
¡Ora lo verás cuando mire
A tu mom!

Límpiense el zoquete
Before you come in!

Y todos en filas chuecas
Pasan pa'dentro
Y antes de que
Se cierre la puerta
Llegan otros dos que andaban
Por allá correteando la yegua
De Don Sostén y apenas
Entran a tiempo

Y se cierra la puerta
Y descansa la yarda
De la escuelita de la sierra —
Gentil cuna de los vicios
Y de la virtud —
Descansa, y al rato
Se empiezan a oir los sonidos
De aquel alrededor serreño —
El chiripio de los chontes
Los lamentos de las tortolitas
Y los alaridos de una cabra.

Y por allá por la placita
Ladra un perro
Y el ruidoso trigal
Al otro lado del cerco
Suelta un suspiro
De compasión — o será
De alivio — ¿Quién sabe? — Pero canta
El silencio al pie del monte.

ESLIPPING AND ESLIDDING

If
You
Are presently
Shifting
And shuffling
Eslipping and
Eslidding,
As we say

And
Leaping without
Looking

And
Alighting
In strange and
Disconcerting
Places and
In even stranger
Positions — try
Not to fret!

Laugh it off
So you don't
Lose the magic
That insures the madness
Which will see
You through

And once that happens
The positions and
The strange conditions
Will have meaning

And you will know
Precisely
What to do
With what
Is left

Which won't be much,
The process having
Been brutal and
Calculated, hasn't
Left too much
That is pure — a mountain
Top here, a new
Island there — not even
New, really, merely
A high spot on the road to the sun

But that,
And your madness
And your
Impeccability — how
You have
Spent your days

1976

Dealing with
The shifting
And the shuffling
Will be all
There is in
The end
And
In the
New beginning

1976

YORE'S DAYS

Where now, all those
carefree, drunken, brawling
days of balling? Agone?

¡Yo digo que no!

Que me faltan más travesuras —
cosas to look ahead to — y chance
que hasta más
exciting que
las de anteayer.

At any rate,

I'm wide open for more, not
of yore, pero algo más o
menos interesante.

And I proclaim,

¡Vámonos recio! Porque falta
mucho y lo mejor del hueso
hasn't been knawed at, yet!

!Ajúa!

THE PARADOX OF LONELINESS
. . . IS THAT IT IS CONSTANT

You can actually forget
loneliness, but only
momentarily and always
in times of stress

And because you sing and
you travel far from home,
because those songs have
to be sung to delight people
and make them forget,
loneliness you find yourself
alone, alone.

And towards the end of
every sojourn you begin
to relax, and you begin to
feel restless and an urgent
anticipation builds up
inside your gut to get back,
to get back home!

But being alone, one can
only look forward to more
loneliness —

Because there is no home
when one is alone. And
that perhaps explains why
so many of us wind up
embracing ugly people.

MUJER SIN FE

Cuando el tiempo llegue
y detenga por sí tu vuelo
te darás cuenta, en ese
instante.

Se desolverán tus penas
que hasta ahorita te
hacen falta.

Y empezarás a comprender
lucídamente por qué te a
negado la vida.

Sabrás por qué sigues
en busca de aquel mito
que no te ha dicho que
ya eres completa — eres
completa.

SOLEDAD

Tristeza ansiosa
¿Con qué fuerzas te contengo?

¿Con qué poder, ansiedad
sofocante, te detengo
antes de que me envuelvas
en tu montaje de luto?

Las noches son las peores.
Y cuando la lluvia cae
siento que casi rompes
las aldabas de
mi santuario.

Sólo dos dulces recuerdos
me sostienen. Y esos
recuerdos preciosos,
ansiedad terca, me salvan
de tu rostro fúnebre, aunque
iluminan también mis
penares.

PORTFOLIO II

Pachucos y Pachucas—Chicano freedom fighters ahead of their time
Cholos y Cholas—la resistencia continues
Juntitos—los dos through thick and thin
Wars—we've been in all of them hoping to end 'em forever

PACHUCOS

PACHUCOS

PACHUCOS

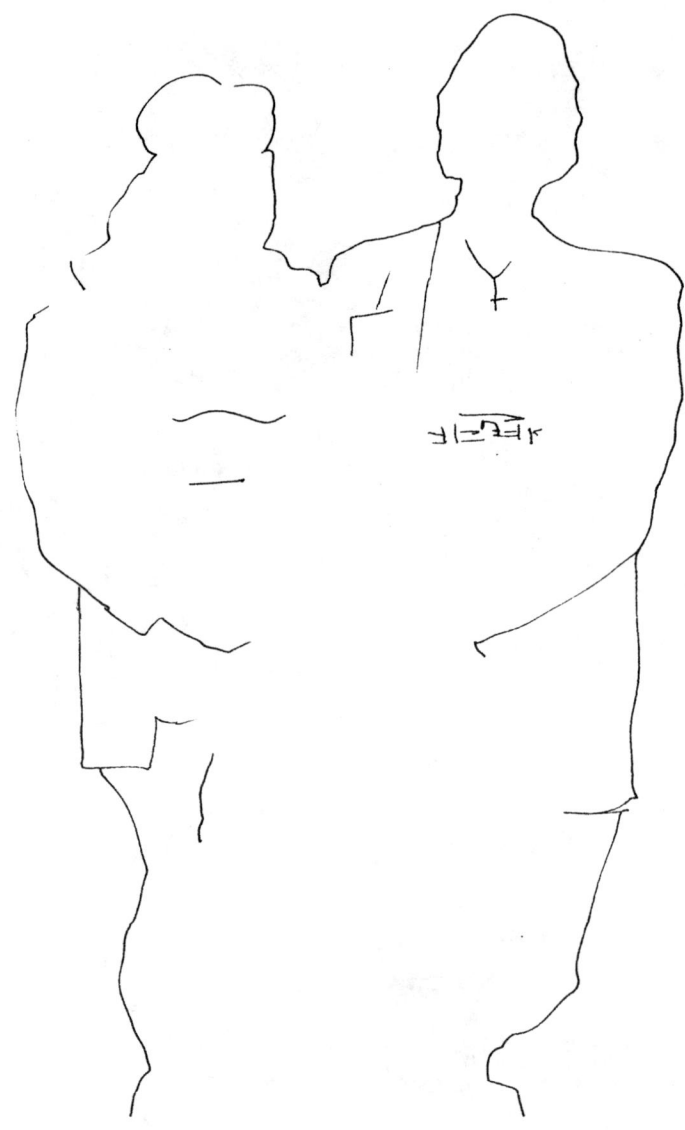

PACHUCOS

PACHUCOS

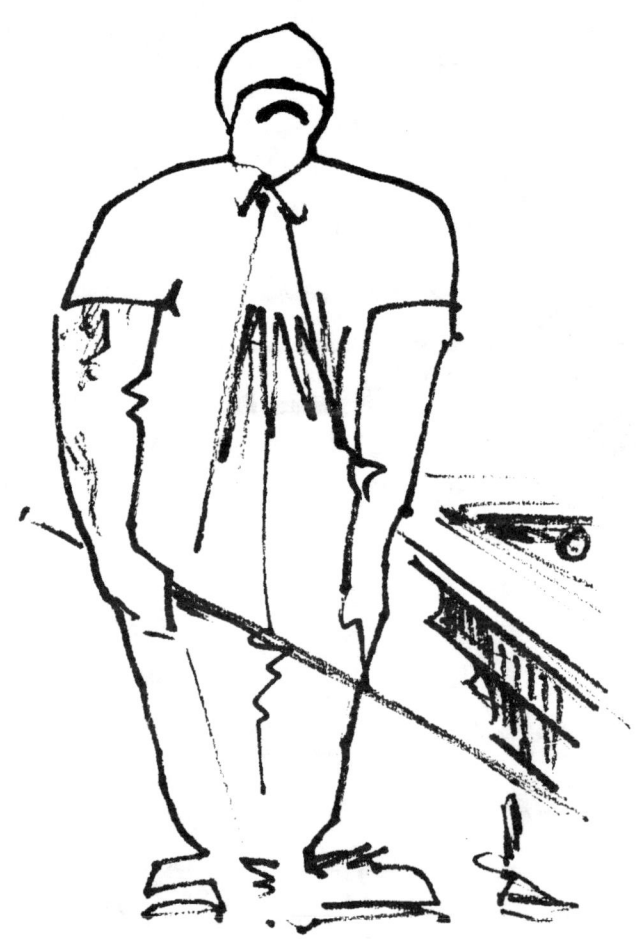

CHOLOS

CHOLOS

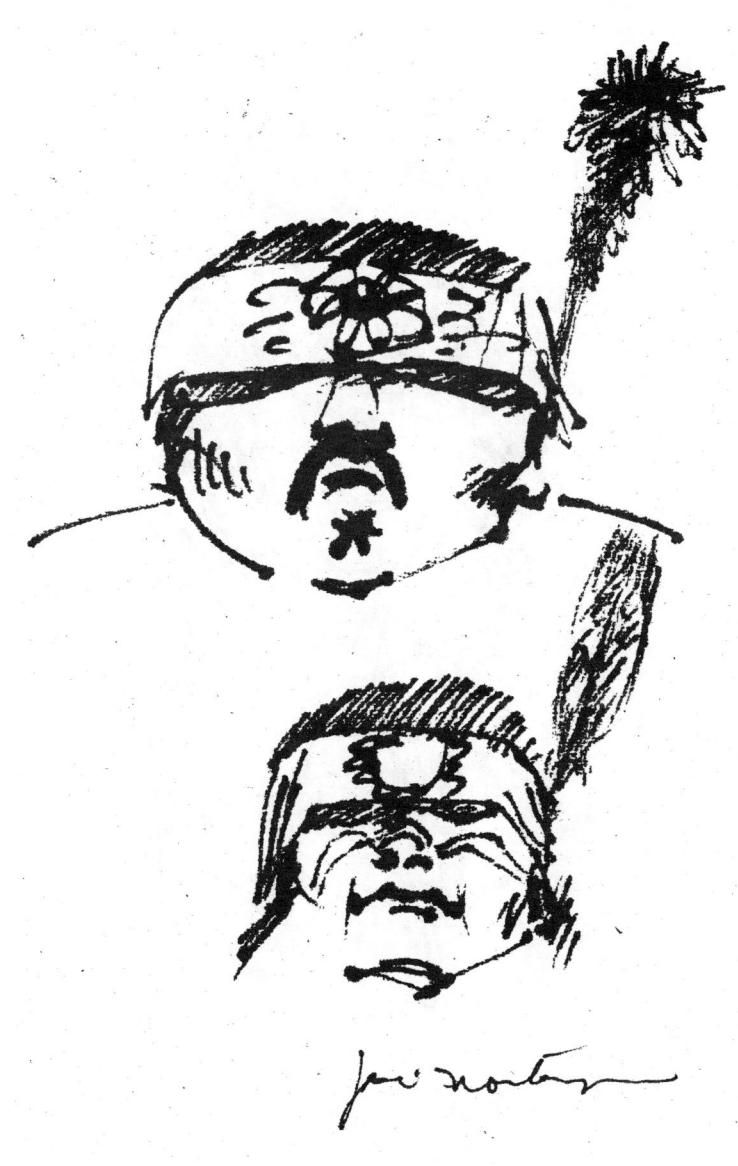

JUNTITOS LOS DOS

WARS AND WARRIORS

LOS THEYS ARE US

We were once a principled people
Ser chuecos was never our style

Los chuecos were always los otros —
Los they!

Now we discover que los they nos
¡¡¡Vacilaron!!!

And striving to build a Chicano
Nation that proposes to guarantee
The Indians a better deal is no
Longer the issue when we consider
Que los theys have Eskimos guarding
The Alaskan pipeline.

Los they beat up low riders like
They beat up pachucos before

But only the uniform is the same —
Porque las caras are our faces!
Chicano cops kill us killing ourselves!

Antes los they used to put us in
MR classes — today they do it in
Two languages.

Only the system remains the same,
But the faces are our faces!

(NEWS ITEM) — Front page, of course!
CHICANO EDUCATOR ABSCOMBS
WITH PROJECT MONIES
(Y saben retorcer el filero)

Noted Chicano educator, respected
Chicano educator!

Before, los public defenders nos
Mandaban al tavique and today, once
MEChA militants are sending us up,
And charging us for it.
(An interesting aside!) There was
A fundraiser for David accused of
Blowing up the telephone company.
His attorney — early movement vato —
Had the audacity to come to where
The barrio was raising the fee — and
David was doing time. (Just an
Interesting aside.)

Y los políticos used us as they
Broke bread with our leaders,
And they lied to us like politicians
Lie, and today the lies are the
Same as we break pan dulce and have

1977

Canela clatches —

And the faces are our faces and
Brown-elected officials make and pass
Laws to destroy us and Panama!

Once we were principled people.

Today we have very little left that
Is still ours — today we have nothing
To lose.

Only confusion can contain us.
Dispel the confusion, compañero,
Y trucha con los they
Cause los theys are us, ¡ése!

1977

IN THE GAZE OF A BLACK EAGLE

In my lifetime
Early on, I began
Hearing of you, ese,
And wondered what
Took you so long.

My compa Villa mentioned
He knew you from the CSO
En Bakersfield,
Not San José, so I knew
You were for real.

. . . I had some things to
Tell you, ése . . . things
I knew you would
Appreciate. I had some
Important data, ¿ves?
Having had undergone
Three years before
The transformation de
Las piscas de Fresno
¡Al existencialismo
De Telegraph Avenue!

So, cocky, I joined
You at the park in
Stockton, and
I found there

Were several
Hundred of us there to
Tell you something you
Should know only to
Find out you honestly
Already knew it — so some
Stayed on anyway, others
Left hurt and infuriated
At your audacious behavior
For such a humble, little guy

The march was confusing
To a lot of us, carnal,
Black captains de SNICC
Y gavas de las marchas
De Alabama y los Busto
Brothers y los toiliros
On wheels — era un carnaval

And you were forever
Surrounded by throngs of
Clergy, Marxists and
Celebrities de todo
El mundo who resented you
Not staying with them
At a travelodge

Twice you acknowledged

1977

Me and lowered your gaze
And I understood that to
Mean you would tell me later.

And I marveled at
Your wisdom and at your
Humility. And I stayed on

And I was with you
At the gates of Freeport
In time to celebrate
The crucifixion and the
Jubilation over the
Capitulation of Schenly.

On Easter Sunday llegamos al capitolio
And in a Sacramental gesture you
Let me help lead the multitudes
Right up to the front of the
Marble steps and I, in reverence,
Bowed my head to the originales
As they filed by on their way
To the front.

And since then, I've fought
Alongside you in all the
Subsequent battles with
Respect and with dedication.
We triumphed together

Con la veinte y dos
And we got whipped
En la catorce —
Y así, hasta que
Salieron los goons
A correr de los files.

But of late, I've been
Concerned, brother, y te
Quisiera hablar de los
Campesinos de Tejas . . .

Te quisiera hablar de
Palestine and
To hear from you
What visiting with Don
Marcos y su ruca
En las Filipinas
Has to do with Gallo
Contracts en Modesto.

So, not unlike the walking days
Of '66, I've been rehearsing
In my worthless, albeit wiser
Head, another message
I feel compelled to take
To you once more, César,
Reflect!
Reflect!

1977

UNDER THE SHADE OF A FRUITLESS MULBERRY TREE

Without a doubt, la sombra
del árbol del centro de artístas
must be considered holy ground
porque allí se mea el Rudy y los
guainitos se embolan y porque
allí se discuten los puntos más
elevados.

Y de allí se ve mi pueblo
de Sacra — pueblo oprimido y
adorado — y de allí también, one
can appreciate the skills of
a people that has learned to
survive a system that has lost
its balance.

Ahí mis hermanos y hermanas
have fenced in this tree of
life, and we sit and we learn
as we witness the church losing
the battle of procurement and
salvation to the street walkers.

And all the scholarly treatises
de San Agustin and Aquinas
fail to show how to deal with
Old Carmen, la cantinera, ex-chuca
who hates priests, pigs, and
other exploiters from long-ago
battles in Chinatown in Fresno,
Southside Stockton y El Reno Club,
as she attempts to make a citizen's
arrest on the decoy at the corner —
"Lady, you're interfering with
our campaign to rid the city of
scum!" le dice el back-up, long-
haired, plain clothesman, "This lady
happens to be a policewoman!"
"¡Es puta! ¿Y tú que? ¡Pinche hippie!"

Y la gente del barrio come to her aid,
"Leave her alone before we call the
police!" " But we are the police!
Padre, tell these people!"

"Mis hijos, mith hijoths!" yells
the priest.

And under the tree we laugh and we cry.
And Louie the foot would never
say that words are fun, but
there he is laughing when Ernie
passes the bottle to Victor and
asks, "Did you ever want to fuck
a placa?" and the phrase is noisily
repeated by all the other guainitos,

1977

"¡Fuck a placa! ¡Fuck a placa!" Until
they realize que la Virgen de Guadalupe
les esta echando ojo from her mosaic
prison y se averguenzan y se alejan
pushing before them their Safeway
shopping carts with all their
belongings and the rotting produce
que recogen en el mercado to sell
for their survival — as if dodging
insensitive juras wasn't enough —

"You're worthless, Ernie! You are
nothing but a goddamn drunk, Ernie,
I get tired of hauling you in!"

"It's just that I take my commitment
seriously, officer, did you ever
see me sober? ¡Hay 'ta pues! ¡Yo
taloneo seguido, compa!"
"That shit's gonna kill you, wait and see!"
"I know that, ése, but do you know
what's going to kill you? ¡Hay 'ta
pues!"

Y se va por la banqueta, algo
holy, entre los alcoholic priests
and the hookers go on hooking
y los johns are jail-bound and
the frenzy continues

Y de allí de la sombra del árbol
del centro we discern las gaitas
y las maniobras de un pueblo
oprimido

And from under the shade of a
fruitless mulberry tree,
se alcanza a ver el nuevo horizonte.

BEAUTIFUL PERFORMANCE AT EVENING TIME

Wispy
Willowy
Tufts
Above the
Early summer
Tree tops
Antics performed in slow motion —
Ever-changing imagery
In white
Against the azure of
Infinite permanence.

And I'm
Sure
I see a sail —
Boat, now
Like any child.

And there, a bolting herd of
Silently
Thundering
Stallions,
Whites and greys.

And now a beautiful bride
In white emerges and fades
And her bridal veil becomes
An awesome

Fish
Form
Leaping
Across
The universe.

Then the fantasy of determined
Blue and fickle white is
Startlingly pierced by a flock
Of black birds
Ushering
Forth
The
Dusk

Transforming the white
To soft pinks
To saddening crimson
Fingers
And the backdrop of
Cocksure
Blue

Blackens and the curtain
Of evening time falls.

THE RIVER

Dedicated ultimately to the earth mother, of course, and to my Raza en general — pero a mi gente de Sacra in particular.

No Mississippi, this one,
no mighty Columbia.
No Snake nor wide
Missouri nor other
rivers of no return.
Not even in competition
con el charco grande
which we lost to the
old cowhand from
the Rio Grand!

Yet, this river does,
in fact, drink up the
waters of the Yuba,
the Feather and the Bear —
and it even swallows up
the mighty American,
this audacious, mischievous
river of the Holy
Sacraments!

    (Har, har, snicker, snicker,
    irreverently, at the audacity
    of the early cross bearers!)

Pero, nevertheless,
éste río de los antiguos
sacramentos del altar
de España is one
mightiful river — at once
calm and reassuring
in its peaceful depths
pero también savage razgadór
de levees and innundator
of deltas — lifegiver/taker,
destructor/provider,
mightiful river!

And if we can maintain
and learn to develop our
tolerance for that river —
and for all humanity — we
will have earned the
right to navigate that
robust waterway past

Mazatlán de Aztlán and
other dangerous straights
all the way to the very
mouth of the Amazón — the
big life-line, big artery,
mainliner's delight, como
las bulging venas de mi

1980

compadre Estevan Villa,
who is himself, verily
like that river!

    Mischievous river, by far
    more spiritual than all the
    holy sacramentos del altar
    de España.

THE CARRION EATERS

Lazy swirls
In the dizzying
Summer skies

Zopilotes
Etching circles
Of innocent
Deception
In the white heat
Scenting/sensing
From up high
The solitary dreamer's
Last ditch effort
To contain
Madness —
Dulce/amarga
Paranoia
Induced
By visions
Too clear to discount —
Too authentic
To distort —
Too real
To suppress!

And from above,
The carrion eaters
Hover ever downward

On blue steel wings
Of total assuredness!

Look upward once more,
Compañero/compañera,
And unleash your lethal
Firepower!
Pierce and shatter
That insidious underbelly
With truth bursts and dreaming
And with your devastating
Filero-sharp gaze
Bring down
The carrion eaters, poet,
And brace yourself
For the next
Assault!

1980

LISTEN

Up in the foothills
Near a strategic
Air command base
On a morning-star dawning
Of a sunrise sweat,
I was gradually startled
Gently by the alacrity
Of a million bird sounds.

Joyous music that had
Penetrated the rigors
Of the burning waters.

And my amazement
Was owed to the
Incredible realization
That the cooing of
Mourning doves, the
Chatter of blue jays
And the shrill versatility
Of the mockingbirds
Had completely drowned out
The more familiar, unnatural
Noises of the B-52s
That in routine regularity
Virtually stun these hills
And beyond, even, all
Of the mornings
Of every day around
This time.

And I was greatly flattered
And thankful, knowing
I was finally re-learning
To hear. Listen!

THE TELLING SIGNS OF DOWNTOWN

There is an irreverent
Disturbing strangeness
To a sight that is
Becoming commonplace, yet remains
Hidden and apart — for now, at least —
From the plight of other
Real and unreal suburban ills.

An unnatural, yet familiar,
Accepted fixture.
Groupings of men —
And of late even women —
Huddled phantom-like,
Shoulders hunched,
Hands pocketed deep,

Surviving, barely,
In the lesser parks
Of the inner-city with alarming constancy
From early in the morning
Through the noon of midday
And late into the darkness.

They trek relentlessly, the route
Of the Sun Father
Across time —
From the Dawn of
    The East

To the dusk of
    The West
Like dog packs
    Beaten
Eyes blurring and burning
    Red
They drag themselves
    Forth
In hopelessness.

And they walk only on
Certain violent streets
Of the inner city
Until they die
Of the irony
Since on any other street
They would obviously perish
So much sooner!

Yet, one can, on occasion,
At that fixed-in-time-forever
Interval, when bottle and lips part —
Just before that
Inevitable, bitter-sweet
    Shudder
That makes the whole body
    Tremble —
At that precise moment,

1981

The ancient, timeless
Aura of the warrior
Flickers in the
Burning eyes of at least some.

And for a flashing
    Instant
The clarity of ceremonial
Burning water
    Cleansings
Reflect visions of once proud braves
And courageous women warriors
Whose ancestors never killed a river
Or violated
    THE EARTH MOTHER
Now, on the violent streets
Of the inner city —
Now, another kind
Of fire water spreads
A veil of crimson
    Spider webs
Across the entire vision.

And momentarily blinded and mercifully
Numbed of feeling,
They go forth, shoulders hunched,
Hands pocketed deep.
They trudge on, on their

Sorrowful journeys along diseased and dying,
Wine-spattered streets,
To yet another park.

All these telling signs
Happening here
In the inner city
As a real/surreal suburbia commutes
Blindly — in at 9, out at 5 —
Determined to affirm and reaffirm
Guiltlessness
In air-conditioned fortifications
Of skeletal steel girders
And high-rise mirrors of reflections
Until it's time to speed away furiously

To the greener parks
Of the four directions
Away from the rotting core of the
Inner city and the telling signs of
    DOWNTOWN.

UN CANTO DE AMOR SERRENO

Montado en pelo
y al pasito
vide en el potrero de la vegita
una potranca retozando.
Y supe que del monte
abajaba un bulto.
Y por la veredita
a la orilla del cerco
te vide bajar
la cuesta
rumbo a la placita.
Traibas dos cubetas
tapadas con trapos
embordados.
Yo detube la yegua
y me escondi
detrás de un encinal
pa' verte pasar cerquita
sin que me miraras.
Y al aprontarte, el saltido
de tus pechos palpitaban
al compás de mis venas hinchadas
con el dolor de los deseos.
Y pasastes y seguí el
ritmo de tus caderas
hasta que tube que resollar.

1982

RENOVATION OF THE STATE CAPITOL

Phallic dome of blinding gold
Your mighty lions of marble
Thrust you skyward
And you stand exposed —
Dry-fucking the cosmic void!
Your nalgas, kneading madly
In a furious swirl
Of white brilliance
Appear to hover
In all that resplendence
Of their own volition!
But wiser teachers remind us
How the earth rejects
Its offenders
Thus, as you may appear
Suspended in glorious splendor
The ultimate truth
Is that the reinforced
Armatures that give your seemingly
Stollied awesome grace
Are nothing more
Than colonnades of lies
To support your dreams
Of nightmares laced with gold
That demand more gold
To appease your
Insatiable lust
While unfulfilled fathers
And mothers rot in anguish
In Folsom and Corona
For violations committed in order
To feed hungry children that can't eat gold!
If we let you —
When you are done with us —
If we allow it —
Our worst fate will merely be
The final assimilation
With the earth.
But your fate — Prick of gold —
For having housed
And given comfort
To the murderers that have reigned
And reposed
And reproduced
The myriad clones of clowns
In your scrotum — for that and
More, you are condemned forever
To thrusting your Sisyphean
Cock skyward for eternity —
Long, long after this Mother Earth
Has quaked her final
Sigh!

DENNIS IS RISEN IN CELEBRATION

I remember him as he was — and
The pain returns this day
On the wings of a mourning dove

Whose cooing blue/grey piquito
Wails a mournful dirge
To the wind

And the wind
In turn swirls
And weaves the sad lament
Into a transparent shroud

That passes through me
And deposits only that grief
Which is mine — then gyrates
Away and over the
Backyard fences del barrio
To make yet more deliveries
Until we learn.

HOW GREAT WAS MY VALLEY

A break in the weather
And a ride in the country
Just to the North awhile

On a sunshining morning
Drenched in early
Spring green

And in the midst
Of all that greening,
GREY.

GREY cropdusters
GREY silos
GREY barns
GREY water-pump towers
GREY!

GREY monoliths,
Monuments to GREED
Stuffed with green —
GREYED dollars
Of rice and paraquat
For Russia
We're told

As if to justify
The nightmare
With sardonic humor, while
The irony
Of the residue
Goes rushing towards

The sea

On gentle/turbulent
Flowing waterways
Gorged with wet winter
Memories to swell the
Rivers and fill the wells
That fill our thirst
With GREY

Just to the North awhile
GREY barns
Great, GREY silos
Spewing a GREY mist —
Smoldering with
The GREY ashes of the Fall.
GREY islands —
GREY on a sea
Of luscious
Growing-green grasses
Glowing
Poisoned
Gasses growing
Growing.
Just to the North awhile
Where the hawks
Still manage, somehow,
To outnumber the cropdusting bi-planes
In the GREY
Above.

EL SOL Y 'L ROVATO LOCO

So there I was
Soaring like poets are wont
To soar
Above and beyond th' trees
And the palms
Going ZOOM
Straight al sol.

    (¡Que suave ser poeta, jefita!)

When on impact
El sunjefe solchief
Exploded — virtualmente
¡Aclarando todo, claro!
Y en la revolcada
I caught glimpses down below
And saw giant
Erector-set vatos, rovatos
Walk-dance energy
Over hills and vales
And mountains
And then I felt
An enormous sorrow
For those children down there.

    (¡Que joda ser poeta, 'ama!)

But the palms

And the pine trees
And the children down below
They just looked up
Past th' metal warriors
Only to see
Battle-ready gunships
Helicoptering South!
South! Right under
Mine bruised
And the solchief's own
Noses!

A DAY OF INFAMY

Today,
Doce de octubre
Día de la Raza
Columbus Day of pain
And glory,
Hoy,
Muy tempranito
Bostiaron, en la Jalisco
Al famoso muerde pan
Sin panic.
And the scourge
De las panaderías del barrio
Dunks stale, hard bread
In jail
Y las empanaditas
Will be whole
And no more toothless
Crescent hits on random
Panes dulces
Y los ositos y cochinitos
Will have,
Once more,
Flanks enteras y 'l pan
De huevo's gonna miss
The gummy signature
¡Del famoso muerde pan
Del barrio!
Happy Día de la Raza,
Raza!
Hell Columbus!
Hail Yes!

TWIN DOUBLE-BARREL SHOGUN

Blast! Blast!
So much gone
macho gone
el machine gone
machine gun next?
¿Quién es
el/la más
chingón/gonna
Be next?
Machine gun
¡me chingan
nos chingaron,
pues!
Los/Las
El macho y las machas
muchas veces,
Broda/sista

P.S. But then, would you
still love me if Julano
Hooligan called me out
and I backed off?

"Heck no, mi'jo — no one
calls this family
welfare bums!"
"Get my sawed-off shotgun!"

1985

IN LAK'ECH ON THE ROCKS

A Manhattan teardrop
Had barely landed on the bar
When Dean Martin
Began booze crooning
Memories Are Made of This
So apropo — just
like a mushy B-film.

A B-film in this day and
Age! Age?

Don't be so sensitive, ese,
Life's a stage, afterall,
Is stranger than
The Bard's own —
And you are nursing
A badly battered heart.

Yes indeed, at your age
On this night of Autumn '85
And April's gone, "the cruelest month,"
Decía T.S., tough shit, Elliot!

Look at it this way,
No, like this!
After tonight you won't be
As forgetful of
Anniversaries or Mother's Day
Or how important backup is

You have to work
At supporting
Your other you.

Ho.

ROUGH TIME IN TH' BARRIO

It was not th' first time —
Budgetary constraints
Had occurred before
In th' early seventies
I remember.

So when I mentioned
The barrio art program
Monies had been frozen
The ancianos were
Very understanding.

They told me not to worry
That things would get
Better and one or
Two of th' feisty seniors
Suggested we make a
Protest at city hall, some
One yelled out — it's the college,
Not the city!
We all laughed and the fact
We hadn't gotten yarn
Was forgotten and we
Steeped ourselves in
Other artsy, craftsy
Projects that night

At the end of class
Luisita came up to me
Grabbed my shoulder
Gently as I was leaving
And looked around and
Coyly but very assuredly
Handed me a brown bag
With a huge slab of
Give-away cheese and
Two, two-pound slabs
Of butter and told
Me not to worry

" . . . take this to your familia
And don't you worry, señor
Profesor — ¡todo saldrá bien!"

Holding back a gasp I hurried out.
I sat in my pickup
And cried for a short,
Guilty, joyous, embarrassing
Instant and quickly glanced
Around hoping the barrio
Wasn't watching my truck

Tough time in th' barrio
In this decade of the Hispanic —
Y la calma Chicano endures.

RAIN

Standin' lonely in th' rain
Sunday lonely 3 pm
Th' laundromat so plain
Th' pain I have wrought so real
And there it was — that deja vu
Sensation. I had felt that rain before —
From Sasebo to say si bone, to say, simón!
In love and in pain
And the smell of the rain
was the only thing
The same throughout
To bail me out.

TH' DOG DREAMERS

Suddenly,
A mean-mouthed pack of dogs
Came out of stage left
Moving across America
In rapacious slow motion
Running funny, they said.
And how they appeared and disappeared
Didn't help, either.
One was a stone, stoic.

The shadow-cloud, dog spectre
Clearly appeared to float,
Propelled forward
Ever so slowly —
Undulating but ever so slightly,
As blithely
As the rhythm of a sigh.
Th' more nearer dog
Was transparent,
Just hovered
And cast no shadow whatsoever.
You could see the mountains
And the horizon right through him.

The third dog-thing
Wore zoot suit pants
And shades — tea-timers
To hide the white of his red eyes

It appeared
And spoke to the house
With the tile roof.

I turned and looked away —
My mouth agape
Wondering if I could even scream.

ALBERT CAMUS' ROACH-CLIP OR SYSIPHUS CON MULETA

Within the poets' bag
Of magic/madness
There is a poem
For the damaged dream
As beautiful as the one
For the dream fulfilled.

DRESS DOWN

Don't go to court
Wearing only your underwear.
Avoid them midnite busts!
Avoid them midnite busts!
It might be raining out there.
Cold dark!
You gotta be
Dressed for it! Make it hard
For th' judge to decide.
Yep! Foul weather gear
At all times is the word,
— no more dumb chancing allowed
'cuz
Reckless abandon
Produces réques
¡Abandonaus, ésos!
So watch your craft
If you're merely studying your craft,
If you're barely studying
Your craft — learn to learn
It right!! An'ehn — An'ehn,
And then share it — share it
With the right people —
Don't squander it,
There can't be no more dirty chonies out
There, ese,
No more sand-blasted skivees.
Dress down!

PORTFOLIO III

It takes more than blind faith, but it does work, sometimes
So does humor work, cause it's rough in occupied Aztlan
El disfraz behind the mask of oppression
La joda y la lucha continue—with love

BLIND FAITH

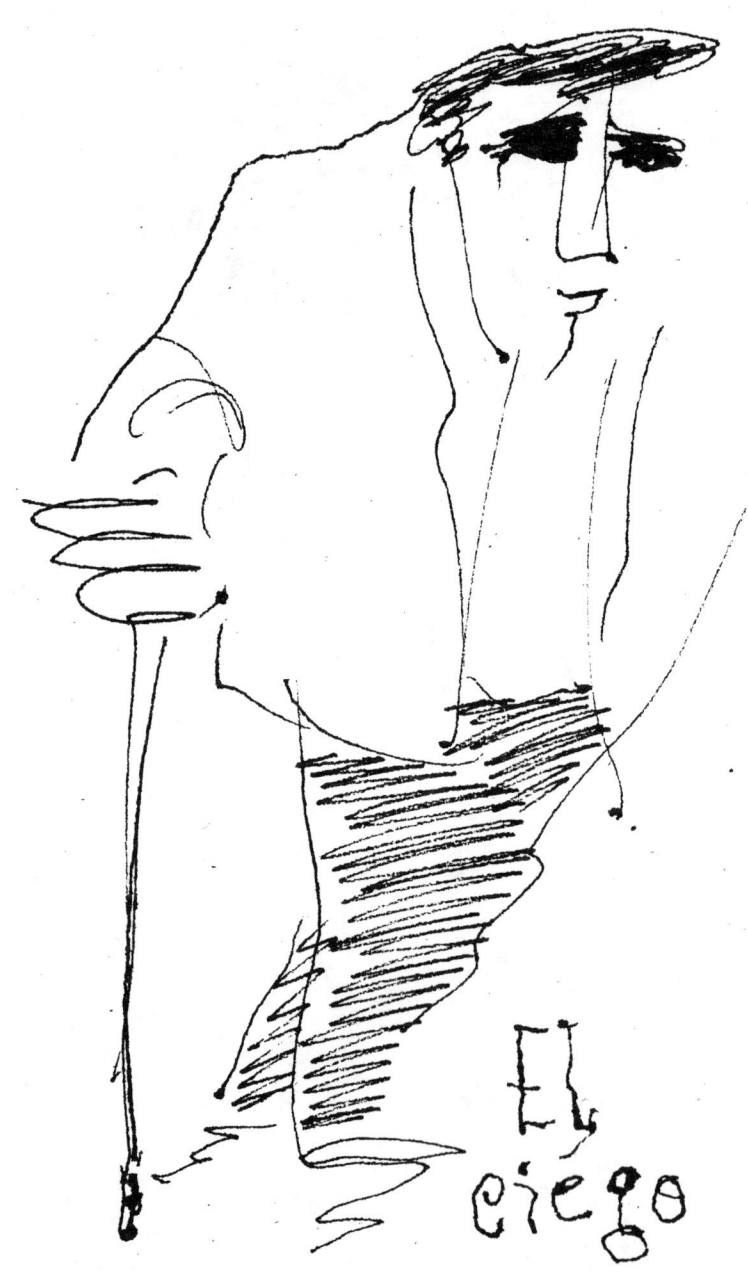

MASK OF OPPRESSION

MASK OF OPPRESSION

MASK OF OPPRESSION

MASK OF OPPRESSION

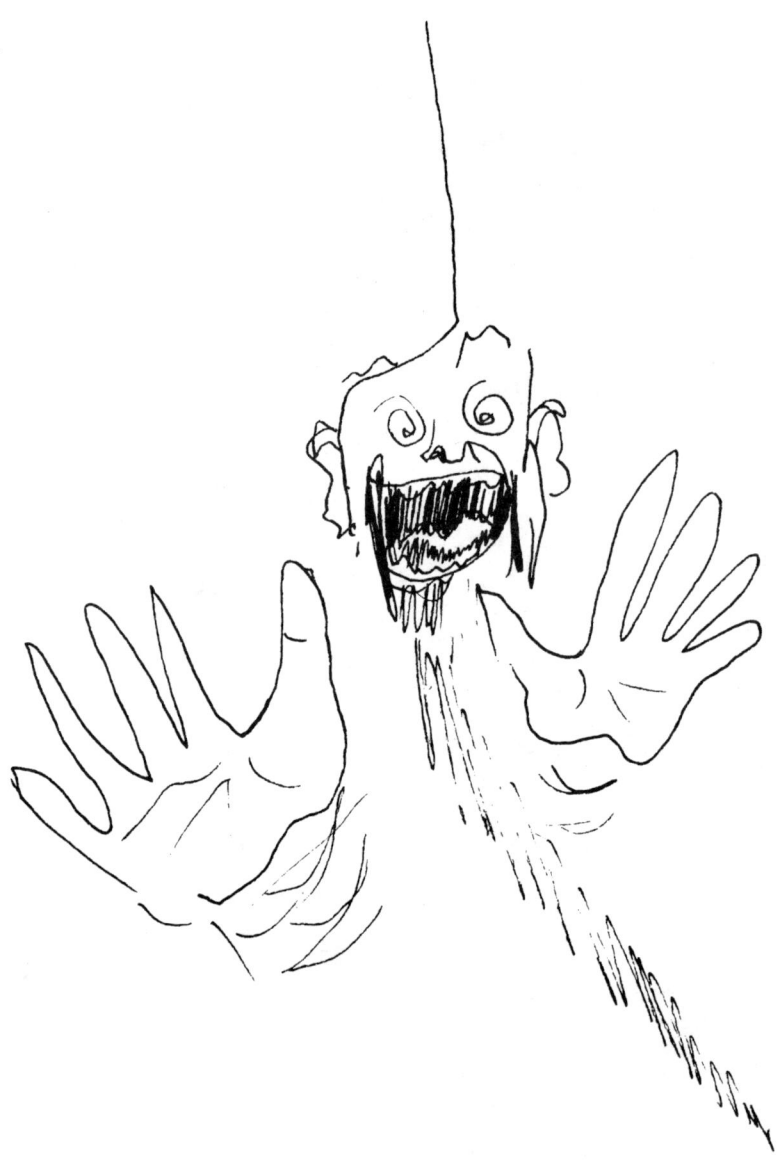

MASK OF OPPRESSION

MASK OF OPPRESSION

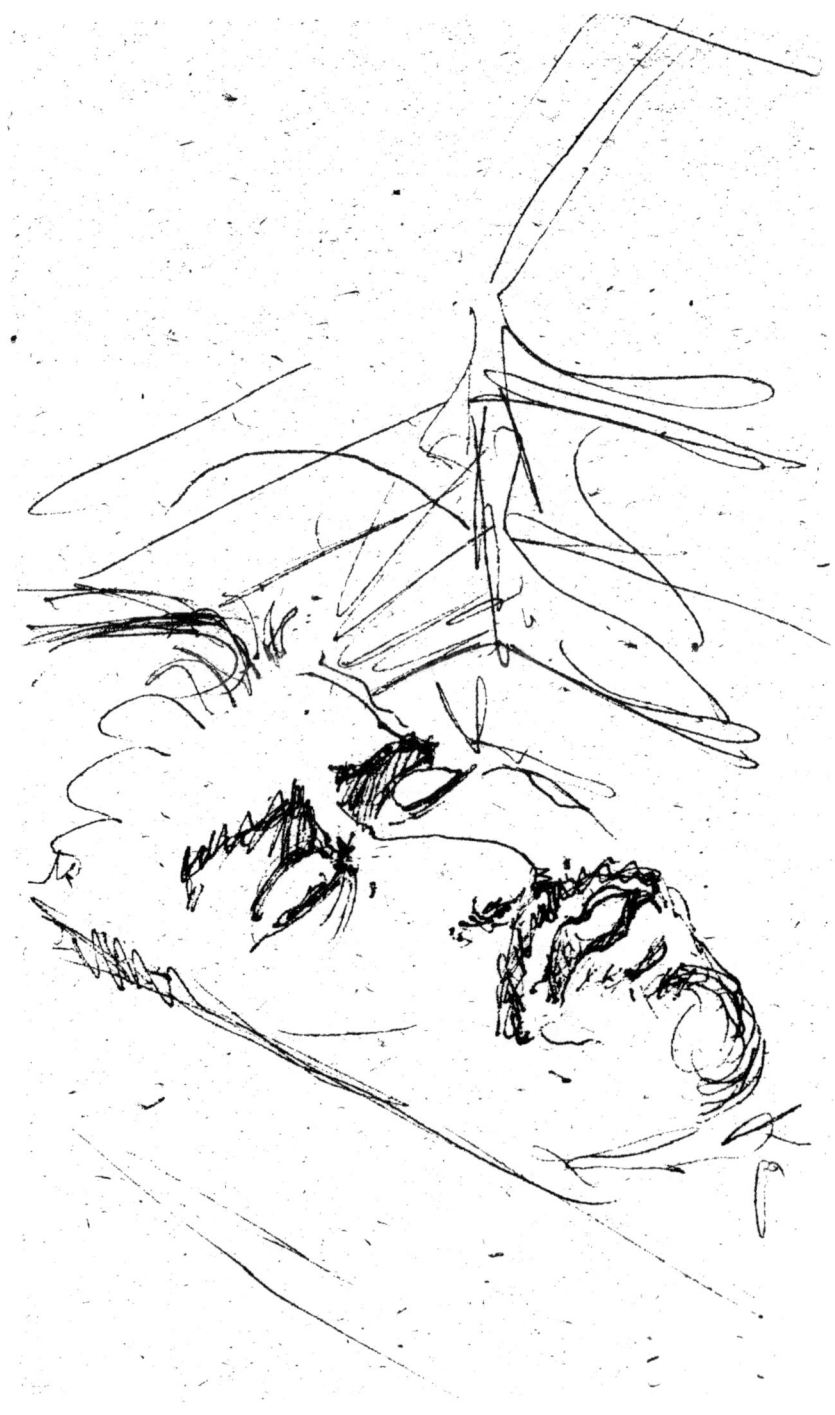

LA JODA Y LA LUCHA CONTINUE

LA JODA Y LA LUCHA CONTINUE

A WAY OF LIFE — A WAY OF DEATH

In the back barrio alleys
Where wainitos die daily
Of the malaise del país
And the race ends in blood
There is still honor in some deaths.
Deaths to mangled bodies
With healthy minds, still —
El Ernie was being bold
Being Chicano again
And he was told to get fucked.
Being the bard of wit
Among barrio bards that are witty
He defends his pride in what he is
And tells the teller
Of the fuck you that he doesn't like
What the practice has done to the teller
And the teller swings one blow
And Ernie falls and dies of the heart
He dies of the heart
Y se va, se va por la vereda tropical
La noche plena de quietud
Con su perfume de humedad
and the music builds and builds!
MOTHER — your son is home!
Ho!

1987

CINCO DE MAYO POEM FOR '87

Getting listos con listas for another Sacra 5
Won't say cinco much longer!
Actually I had a whole array of reasons
For this journey of poetic journalism —
Reportaje nouveau — antiguo de novedades paradojicas
But here we are readying for
Recreating — even replicating La Battalla de Puebla
One more time and seeing Napoleon still triumfando
Y el Chicano pierde su voz to an ironic proposition
Just as downtown Sacra begins to look like Paris
Now that the light-rail project is nearing completion.

And the eye of th' artist can't help but yearn
For th' showers of April when this Parisian downtown
Of mine most assuredly will be transformed
From memories of th' ol' 'K' Street
Of two-way traffic to the recent media-fest of battle grounds
And concrete pyramids of reinforced steel
Complete the 'K' Street obstacle course of th' seventies
And the chief and th' merchants and politicos
Blaming the cholos from downtown barrios
For most of th' chaos, to the
Present now of tree-lined, cobbled-brick streets
And trolly rails and a background
Of Guccied-down ladies and a host
Former activist (agents of change)
In three-piece body bags pretending hard
In an effort to handle th' malaise.

1987

Pobrecito Benito Juárez — Poor Bennie Juárez
Or Bennie who or perhaps numbers will save us!
The confusion continues as before when
Benito rode the hills of Puebla
And Oaxaca in a black carroza wondering
Who was intervening — who was coming for him.
¿Cómo estubo, Don Chepo?
Pos, a Don Benito Juárez ya le daban las tres,
¿Serán los Mexicanos o será el ingles? 'sabe?
Al pobre Bennie Juárez ya le daban las tres,
¿Serán los españoles o será el francés?
¿Quién fue, Mamá Carlota, quién fue?
Pues fue el francés 'apá. Sí, fue el francés
Con la ayuda de un gabardin como Rin Tin Tin.
Le dice a Zaragoza, pues ya sabes quién es.
Encamínale la pompa y mándame las tres
Las tres personas, 'amá,
Las responsables, 'amá.
¡Pobre México! ¡Fijisi, disque fue un garbardín!
An actor was at it way back then!
Wasn't he a dog,
Someone asked?

WHERE'S YOUR FACE, ACE?

Looking here and ove' yonda'
Where's your
Face, Ace?
Well, now ain't
It a wonder
Yes, indeed
Where's your face, Ace?
Find it Ace
And wear it well
An' don't you
Lose it
Like I lost mine, once.
But I'm looking, Ace
I'm a looking and
I'm thinking and I'm re-thinking
Yea! Where's your face, Ace?
Let's go looking
One and all!
Got to have face, Ace
Before we start
The hard search
For the heart
Ace.

ONE CASINDIO'S REACTION TO THE MEDIA

Outrage pure and simple!

How dare the Premier say
we are inferior!
Sounds like Hitler or
some racist social scientist

Outrage!

Pure and simple! Yeah!

Why, the nerve of that purist pig!

Blinding outrage, to be sure!
Still,
one must remember that
one's dignity
demands fairness which
compels honesty
and other considerations
that lead to examine
one's own indignation —
indigenous indignation,
if you will, at a carnala
marrying a black man
or a carnal marrying a white lady —

confused rage, pure and simple!

Because there are those other
recollections and the memories
of English Pubs in '43,
Seoul, Yokasuka, Manila
1950's Chicano GIs and
nostalgic Korean warrior loves
are provoked because
we did love, dig?

We loved so intensely!

But our commitments to our own
were obviously more intense,
if not our love
so we used those cultural commitments
as excuses to disconnect.

But those things never quite
disconnect entirely.
Just enough perhaps,
and we lose love.
In whatever subtle measure,
we divest
ourselves of dignity!

Indigenous dignity, dig?

Where is the outrage then?

1988

CRACK

The myth begins to crack
with every crack amidst
th' clamor of the Hispanic
mandate — you can strive but you
musn't struggle, it proclaims.

But Chicanos have been called
a people steeped in paradox
labeled that by an inconsistent
sociedad — consider th' following
contradiction — one of Ronnie's
'nother high-court picks
gets busted mariguandering
'round them hollowed halls of
justice!

Justice!

Just us an 'em again!
    Could be th' signal, folks!
    Could be th' signal!

Cause the parade of justices
goes on for th' right judges
    Ja jez!
    Ya ves!

Y ahí está la pinchi Nancy
teaching us to say no —
como una jefita, ése
while Ronnie an' Ollie
an' th' big chair cut deals
with th' traffickers
to seal the Chicano pogrom
and the Barrio dies
in th' free-based fumes —
gesticulates and cracks
with crack as th' Contras smirk
and shift th' spotlight away

and the country's main G-man
eez'n big trouble his meeself, Bro,
and a corrupt wall-street tail spins
y el P.T.L. ya no pita
¡hijo 'e puta!

Enough to make Chicanos panic!
And also wonder
if and how they have aided
and abetted — and they begin to talk
and to think — and begin to return —
some, at least — because now
worse that ever before
begins th' persecutions
of just us.

1988

of th' different — us
of th' defiant — us
of th' dying — us
of th' Indians — us
of th' poor — us
of th' dopers — us
of th' gangs — us
of th' Chicanos — us

— am I an us you ask? Just
ask the media!

And for just us they have
th' tanks and th' tac-squads
and th' camps are there
ready to be filled by just us
and they will use th' usual
fascist tactics — and ratting
children!

Pretty vicious stuff
while our best minds atrophy

same madness as before of
beatitude times — but who
hears this "Howl"?
Will the present Ginsburg
with a you

and Noriega an' th' Meeses
to pieces and Ron an' Ollie
and that gang finally
embarrass us enough
to cry and not to die? Yeah!

    Could just be
    the beginning —

Th' beginning of a new deal —
real healing, healthy attitude
towards those herbs that heal —
an' nature will again see
pine trees cone naturally
'round green blue-lakes with
real water not acid.

    Could just be a
    good time for a
    respite — a rest

A rest and go then,
instead, inspired! Go inspired
after the real menace
like th' madness of love
being death—of smac
and cocaine.

1988

And Ronnie's regime
with its warped script
and its cast of dopey characters
will go to wherever
people go to pay
for crimes against humanity.

If we — just us — strive
and struggle and
don't crack!

1988

A CLEANSING/UNA LIMPIADA

O limpia
oh limpiada
¡las oo limpiadas!

No gold for th' chumps
only change for th' champs.

Our marathon goes on—¡el maratón!
    de mis hundred-yard dashes
    always under th' record
    y las long-distance races
de tu memoria que nunca
    descansa — ¡qué aguante!

And my enfadosa habit of forgetting
as soon as my short distance
spurt ends at th' tape

    And on to th' next dash
    and th' coaching and th'
    conditioning you help set-up
    for my victories —

Certainly seem for naught —
not a sura word, like aún, quizás,

    so let me from
    now on

thank you before
th' race
begins
not ends!

. . . and don't sit there
and wait for me to say —
    when did I say that?
    I forgot!

1988

THE XURA CURA TRIBE REPORTS

On the eve of
Good Friday '86
good time to say
back from France!

    ("volvió de Francia — engasau!"
    An earliest of childhood sound
    recollections of World War I
    in the mountains of New Mexico.
    I am that old! That young!)

Perhaps that explains why
the should-a could-a
could-a should-a blues
have settled in —
I should of done this
done that!
Could have — no excuses.
Should make effort to say
about what I did do,
could!

But rather, there was so much,
so much one could say
y muy facilito
with the Fox's expertise
one could even
build a case against

the Shooda-Cooda Blues.

But let me at least
relate unas cuantas light ones
de esos ocho días
with el Monjo they
all called my Boswell
and he replied, Qué sura,
Monsura en París — comiendo
y comadriando en el cantón
del picador Picasso.
All that — yeah!
and a day and a night
in London's Heathrow
Airport — stranded — making
camp and sharing
in the lobby
with African tribe migrations
Hindus n' Arabians
Gunga Din 'n Aladdin,
Tin Tan y su carnal Marcelo.

But that really makes it only one
of several light ones.
I have promised you
Parisian tales with Rafas and Jaime
Un Chicano y su primo de Chicali
casindios en exile

1988

and that foggy, folly, London one.

First en Francia, Monsieur
Au contraire! Au contraire!
I had waited fifteen
maybe eighteen years
certainly since
the good ol' dizzy daze
de los cantos
del artístico Reno Club
movement madness days of the sixties
to say, au contraire
to some French intellectual
¡y en francés, ése!
Knowadamean? ¡Sí señor!

Au contraire, ¡mes amigos
del sewer de la
gran Europa! Au contraire!

¡Me di vuelo!

But I should say it
like I saw it
Could!
Should!

Because the French experience
happened intensely and was
constant throughout the entire
tiempo we were there
invited, sin embargo
to correct some false impressions
los europeos might
harbor 'bout who we are
y me da tristeza sad to say
that some of my Xicain colegas
did little to dispel and
correct — representatives from
two different Razas
Unidas can indeed be as
confusing as bad-rapping
the Bourgie set-up and then dining
with the enemy at th' American Embassy.

Les Chicains, Monsieur,
qu'est-ce qui se passe?

Pues, ah — well er . . .

Mon surro Poet Chicain
eeza yohoor mouvemont
ded?

    Hummm
That's the deadest way

1988

I've heard it put, Pierre
I mean, it kills it
ded!

Pues va pa' ded when
two Hispanic Ph.D.s
el Hispanic, ella, unsure or al revés
at best confused always-the-more
never-the-less — there the two
cutting low a Chicana's
literary efforts, sacando garras
al balcón in doctorese, with ease
over there, sans criterio
Chicano, only gets them off
the two and leaves the rest
angry and unfulfilled, confused.
Au contraire.

As contrary as hearing a treastise
on Andy Warhol's 15 minutes
of fame for a couple of
New York sprayers — good bread
and off the Campbell Soup lines
is poor arithmetickling results —
Two or three grafitos out of a thousand or so
del cuchi frito corridor is sad!
As sad as impressions left
en Paris that altares

celebrate death in Chicano Art! —
A paper 'bout a demise
whose time is not yet.

But the violence, mon ami, pour quoi?
Our violence, as our murals
will tell you, is sacred — and plumas
reverse the versos, versus that,
versus this, or the other.
Y el alma de la Raza with
a studio in Maui c'est une tristesse,
monsieur, es tristeza
and it ain't Marxist no more
no matter how well we
served our César y la paz en La Paz
¡pero chále con la tristeza, Pierre!
L'Art Chicain no es mort
Au contraire! Il vive! Vibra!!
Check it out!

Chicano posters en los muros
de la mansion — our plaqueazo
in Paris indelibly
etched in the minds of
the good folks of Europe
the Germans, the Britons,
the Italians... Ay, Amalia —
obnoxiouse romantic that I am —

1988

¡me encanique!
What about the real Hispanics, though?
We'll see in Barcelona in '88
Barcelona?
Ho — where is the Chicano going now!
How prepared am I to return
to my partial origins? Enough for now.
Let's remember the bunkers of Germershiem
and how we gave in Paris
Yes, airlifted Germany of '48 in '84
was clean and orderly, squeaky clean, and
the squeaks were getting louder
suddenly from the ground
from in th' ground
behind those lovely slopes
with the rows of vineyards
embroidered mit ordum
came American jets!
And the squeaks and the countryside music
were devastated —
But it was good to make good friendships
there with folks that hear beyond
the decibels — and I may be wrong
but I heard support from both blocks
two blocks away against the
Hispanization of Indios, Chicanos!

But we were beaten from within!

And before we could march
triumphantly into Paris —
to the disdain of many and the relief of some —
we had lost the east bloc scholars
and had taken on wormed wood
from Miami!
¡Q-vo Cuba!

Then I hear Favela say
let's get the sheep outta here
and in London we saw it —
The white is fading, ese!
London is coloured!

I say moite, why izzat?
(Waited since WW two to
say that — no intellectuals
at Heathrow — only Bobbies
that sounded like Ringo Starr.)

And one crazy Briton poet
being escorted off the premises
yellin' "Rue th' fokin'
poet wot cunt
spell mussy"!

Oy say wot? I mimicked
cheerio 'n all that rot, eh!

1988

Eh rut, mite! Whed'ja loin it?
I couldn't resist it — waited too long.
Khyber Rifles, moite,
Korea '51 — I had passed myself off
as a Kippling fighter de la Queen!
Cheerio, moite!

Down there in the fog where
the white is fading
London's Bridge is falling
and it doesn't cross
me over to Broderick
and Bryte where the cholos
de los barrios are lighting up
the skies.

Back from France!
Could! — Should!

Hay tiempo to return
from Paris
and to return to reason.
    Should — Could!

1988

AÚN

Ay, manito, aunque el dolor
y el dólar continue to
weigh us down
el peso pesa y a uno
le duele.

Y al dolerle a uno
nos duele a todos.

I am still Chicano
habitante aún de
la Chicanacíon Casindia
lidiando sin y con papeles
pero con pipa y papiros
a veces to survive
in this land of the
frequent vicious bullies.

Bullying that turns
God Bless America
my home sweet home
to god damn America
my home sin home
where golpes/blows
are daily manufactured
y el golpe that's
calculated and aimed
at México no le alcanza —

No le llega — falls short
and lands on my head
on my Chicano head
time after time after time.

Y aún the phony
diplomatic ties
are maintained, at
my bloody head's
expense.

Y mi gente de la Nueva España and
even my own parents
and their own parents
haven't sensed the pain
leave alone the
magnitude of my blight
de casi ser — pos no sé,
¿Sabe?

Pero seres somos
se sabe
you savvy? ¿Alguien
Sabe? ¡Casi!

Cause we have indeed
conferred Ph.D.s and
other physical disabilities

1988

on our own ambitious few
so that scholars
can define us
scientifically and to
further re-difine us
y nos definen y
nos refinan diario
and daily nos siguen
refinando sin/con salsita
in the schools
in the prisons
in the churches
en los files
in the barrios
in the reservations
y en las sierras morenas
cielito lindo

Y aún seguimos,
casi — porque mientras
haya sol we go
like that — we chose
no Spanish dream. That
nightmare we carry
como castigo bendito
on our shoulders

And thus, my Indian
casi nacionchica existe,
aún — mired in the
tangled, barbed telarañas
con puias de la red de acero
stretching and scanning
itself on the horizon
where my casi presence
also manifests itself

Aún, seguimos casi
¿Casi y qué?
¡Casique no, casindio si!

Y'al masindio machine
masizo le pedimos
disculpas — así somos — Chicanos
que no nos dejen caer
Ahh! sí somos — casi
pero ay ay ay que bonito son
que bonitos son los feos

Y aún que tanto
u tantito nos duela, Raza,
we shouldn't be
so melancholonized —
ya estufas con estar
tan melancolonizados, ¡Aún!

1988

THE UNIFORM OF THE DAY

    Strong and bold
they came — alone, in teams,
    droves — early on
to sociologize us an' to
    weaken us.

    One day
there they wuz — in the barrio
    studying th' points, us —
y nosotros estudiando el punto
    scrutinizing as well
this army of scholars wearing
    corduroy and clipboards
      and audacity huffing and puffing
    crooked briar pipes
an ours of deer horn, stone,
or clay and wood, even —
good pipes, good smoke I miss
    and I miss th' girls
      that loved boys, women
    men, and went on
      some even to graduate school.

. . . and my colega that has become
invisible on campus that I miss
from old action days now I see
on Saturday mornings strolling
there lonely in th' uniform.

Corduroy jacket with elbow patches
clutching a pipe, brow
furrowed deep, suffering —
    yet, digging his latest
    findings, enjoying his resaerch,
    walking his Cocker Spaniel.

. . . why is that sound so succulent?
Spaniel — Spaniard — Hispanic, Hispaniel?
    Well, every uniform should have
    a dog — I myself walk the derelict dog.

An 'en there's my own trapos —
my uniform de la calle — boogies
(baggies) khakis o gabardine o
sharkskins, gauchos en el
summer, workshirts for th' cold —
blue, cotton or Pendleton
and if colder my blue Sir Guy jacket,
calcos del fil
or Rockport bisquits
for diabetic feet y mi tapa
Stetson Beaver stingy brim
or watch cap!

    Now if that ain't a uniform!

And how absurd that

1988

uniform must look on
Campus!

    As out of place as
    corduroy and briar
    pipes in th' Barrio

. . . but that's what the contract
called for, muy conformes
    in uniform.

HISPANIC NIGHTLIFE AT LUNA'S CAFE WHEN TH' MEXICANS CAME TO VISIT TH' CHICANOS IN CALIFAS

It is a well known fact
that in the education we got
from the Chicano movement
we discovered, affirmed,
confirmed and reaffirmed
our "Indianness."

No sooner had our indigenismo
emerged fuerte y sano
from healing enjuagadas,
cleansing and re-cleansing y mas
que fue reviviendo la
conciencia europea — that same
conquista attitude que
habiamos mandado a la madre
con Cortés y los Malinchistas
¡pero la mera madre nos/los
rechazó!

So today the struggle within
our Mejicanidad es una
lucha antigua entre lo Indio
y lo Europeo — and from
there the struggle/joda
vacillates entre Chicano/Hispano
Mejicano/Indio y hasta Latino
eres tú, bruto!
Quo Vadis, Chicano?

Me pregunta un cuate firme
de Tepito.

Y le digo al Chilango de
la capirucha, que that's what
the Chicano needs to know
in Tewa or Apache
o hasta Azteca — a dilemma?
¡Tú dile, ma!

So the lines are drawn
and it's not an Apache
or even an imperious Aztec
or a Tewa or two against
some Moor in Spain from Africa
or a Visigoth from up North.
It is about those of us
who are neither from
Mayan splendor nor Iberian
Gypsy—We who didn't
make it whole but almost,
casi—were not ni Moros
ni Negros, ni Blancos,
somos más, Casi!

So the Casis, then, are
the ones on the line —
Casindios on one side

1989

Casispanos on the other
los Casindios in their struggle
siguen al Masindio Masiso
y su Masisa de maíz
and the Casispano also
pronounced Cathispano by
the guey, venerate
al Machine y la Machine
sin rin ni matachín!

Solo casi nos queda
que nos libre
san Tin Tan
en calo
Ho!

1989

A CHICANO VETERANO'S WAR JOURNAL

The A. P. photo on the front page
of the violence during the
elections en El Salvador
stuns all the sensibilities!

¡Chingao, carnal!

Ah-ummm-silence screams
in the mind! Four for four
and the circle around it!

Sad to think that today's
Chicanitos and the youth in general
have only that photo to measure
the carnage of war violence —
fueled by — who gives
a damn!

Whether it is greed
or ignorance, it
diminishes us!

And what about those
of us who already
served gallantly — blindly?

Who have in our own
Americanization witnessed

horror scenes too
similar in Viet nam
in Korea — in World War II.
Nosotros, los veteranos,
us! ¡Cabrones!
Where are we?
To tell the youth
the horrible truth
to that A. P. photo —
about our barriadas,
Raza? The violence is here!

El Salvador is our
Barrio, Raza!
And how rapidly we
are letting our barrios become
the violence of future
A. P. war journalism.

1990

A PACHUCO PORTFOLIO

A PACHUCO PORTFOLIO

. . . pa'l Tin Tan y La Toña y su carnal
Marcelo y pa' la memoria
del Che who boogied, de cincho,
and to the memories del Guti Woody
Cárdenas, Agustín Lara
y el Licho y La Ruca.

A PACHUCO PORTFOLIO

. . . a portfolio of ghosts for and
about la plebe del west side
east side south side norte —
for and about us of the cross
and the four directions and
for María Félix —
Ramona Dolores La Googoo y la Tony
La Vicky y amores de las calles —
Los Tríos/Jazz Chicano época
de los forties and fifties —

A PACHUCO PORTFOLIO

. . . del Chuco, Alburque, San Quilmas
y los — "¿Los what?" they would
always ask — and continue asking
to this day, los ask-a-mouse — while
Chicanos went boogie woogie and
hey, Ba-ba-li-ba los mambos y échale
cinco al piano que siga el vasilón —

A PACHUCO PORTFOLIO

. . . y a teoricar acá de este lado,
on this side in Spanish y en inglés
Tewa, Yaqui y en calo,
buti-tirili, de aquéllas, no lie!

A PACHUCO PORTFOLIO

. . . carnalas y carnales, chicaspatas
por vida y bien entacuchados
adding style and class to being
half-breeds who took their Indianness
and Hispanishness and became
Chicanos — ¡los Nuevos Mexicanos!

!qué curada!

. . . ¡ser tirilongo era ser Chicano, ése!
¡Ciról! ¡Al alba, trucha y agusao!
Ya estufas — ¡no sean maje!
¡No monqueén con mis huesos!
¡Cortense sus pedos! ¡Oigan!

1990

A PACHUCO PORTFOLIO

. . . chuco-chuca ghosts in their voices
giving us a bit of our story — his story,
her story in thierstoric fashion, camita,
Chicano history that can't be denied!
And when you make that kind of history
you resent being dehistorified!

A PACHUCO PORTFOLIO

. . . fuck the horrors — ultimadamente,
we are still here — no nos echen
la bendición yet — Octavio Peace, brother,
didn't get us in his labyrinth
and yet was made the nobeler for it!

. . . ¿cómo jodidos que no nos vamos a curar?
¡Orale!
¡La curada!

. . . heal yes, ¡Simón que sí!

A PACHUCO PORTFOLIO

The Songs y Los Corridos

GARBANZO BERET

El día 29 de agosto, señores
el mero día de la marcha
se escribió la historia muy inesperable
de un amigo de la causa

Le decían Garbanzo, no era militante
no andaba en El Movimiento
pero en aquel día de infamia, señores
su valor sirvió de ejemplo

Montado en su Harley se sentía orgulloso
de ver tanto Mexicano
con una botella de birria en la mano
gritaba, ¡Viva el Chicano!

Por la calle Whittier La Raza marchaba
en protesta del gobierno
con puños alzados, unidos gritaban
¡Viva el poder del Chicano!

Al llegar al parque Garbanzo notaba
demasiados policías
le dice a su compa, ésta va a estar pesada
hay que jugarla bien fría

El parque Lagunas parecía una fiesta
una fiesta de colores
quién iba a pensar que esa tarde de amores
se convirtiera en horrores

Garbanzo y la Yuca se estaban sonando
echaos en sus morosiacos
cuando oyeron tiros, gritos y alaridos
todo se volvió un mosaico

Con una mirada quedan en acuerdo
de ir ayudarle a la gente
montaron sus bestias, monturas de fierro
y se lanzaron al frente

Los chotas de pronto bloquéaron las calles
con barreras formidables
Garbanzo en su Harley entraba y salía
azote de los cobardes

Por la calle Whittier La Raza marchaba
en protesta del gobierno
con puños alzados, unidos gritaban
¡Viva el poder del Chicano!

LULAC CADILLAC

¡Órale! 'Scuse me
Hey, it's you
Where you been
Jelly bean
Sorry, man, I didn't mean
I didn't mean
To get you all upset
It's only me

It's been awhile
Que no te veía
Con esos trapos y esa ruca
No te conocía
Now you say
You just come back
To look around
And to say goodbye

Pues no hay fijón
Carnal frijol
Just don't forget
How it's supposed to be
You're gonna lose
It seems to me
Your chile eatin'
Ability

And while you be stylin'
Your best role model

Ya la grandota
Ya se la llevaron
And now she's gone
And you're feeling all alone

And now she's gone
Back to Washington
And she ain't acomin' back
But you're not alone

You see that Low Rider
Crusin' low and slow
Don't let that fool you
It can jump like a jumpin' jack
And it's goin' straight
For your Lulac Cadillac

It's goin' straight
For your Lulac Cadillac
You don't have to give it up, Jack
Why don't you just come back

LOS HUELGISTAS

The year was '73
A time we'll always remember
And in the harvest of shame
The Union never surrendered

Año del '73
Presente lo tengo yo
De aquélla infame cosecha
Y el triunfo de nuestra unión

Los huelgistas en la liña
De Sanger hasta Parlier
Traiban corriéndo a los Teamsters
Y el durazno se pudría

Nos desafeaba un ranchero
Un esquirol y su abuela
Pero nuestro entrenamiento
Fue en el valle de Coachella

Decían los juececitos
No se permiten moquetes
Los huelgistas en acuerdo
Sacándo gente al piquete

Los chotas también dicían
Que no quiren violencia
Pero eran puras habladas
Maltrataban sin conciencia

En los condados de Kern
De Fresno y el de Tulare
No pudieron los cherifes
Tampoco los federales

En eso cambió el asunto
Y empezaron a 'rrestar
Echaron corte parejo
No había pa' dónde arrancar

Perdóname César Chávez
Y la Virgen Guadalupe
Pero antes de que me arresten
Los voy hacer que se preocupen

De la cárcel del condau
Les mando estos cuántos versos
Pa' que se animen huelguistas
Y no aflojen el esfuerzo

Ahí díganle a mi cuadrilla
Y a la oficina de Selma
Que no rompan mi tarjeta
Que ahí les caigo pa' la cena

The year was '73
A time we'll always remember
That in that harvest of shame
Our Union never surrendered

DERELICT DAWG

The derelict Dawg came to my do'
sayin' ese, can you spare a bone
le dije yo, pos sabes que
I ain't got no bone
pero hay arroz y tantitos beans

Me dice el Dawg con un ojo caido
you mean for this
I went and left my barrio
well, I'm aheadin' on back
across the tracks
I'm gonna jam
back to 12th and D

It's just that I
get so doggone tired
of chewin' on them
clean picked, no-meat-left
on-them, slick menudo bones
I get so tired
I get so tired
I could cry

Well, it does look bleak
le respondí
but check this out
before you split
I saw my vecina's daughter

throwin' out the dishwater
and I saw rollin' on the dirt
some chicken-mole bones

Oh, wow! Bow wow!
Me dice el Dawg
imagine that!
chicken-mole bones
this far from my cantón
he did a crazy little shuffle
jumpin' up and down
he wagged his tail
and he boogied
back downtown

Now the very next time
I saw me the Derelict Dawg
venia cruzando los traques
had him a six-pack and his dog mama
and a whole dog pack asingin'
chicken-mole bones
yes, indeedy
they were singin'
chicken-mole bones

EL MARINERO MARIGUANO

Cuando estaba en la marina
me pasaba pa' Tijuana
a ponerle a las quinelas
y a consigir mariguana
pero un día por descuidado
me torcieron en la aduana

Cuando salí de la estaca
me pusieron en un barco
que iba derecho a la guerra
al otro lado del charco
pa' no aburrirme en el viaje
rolé una lata de frajos

El barco era de esos chicos
que les dicen barreminas
son los primeros al frente
y tienen fama en la marina
lástima que el de nosotros
nunca tuvo disciplina

En un borlo en Honolulu
me encontré una borinqueña
bailamos toda la noche
y me encaniqué con ella
de allí nos fuimos a la playa
a jugar allí en la arena

En la costa de Korea
se planiaba una envasión
mandaron los barreminas
a estudiar la situación
por estar rolando un leño
no oímos ni la explosión

Al capitán por borracho
el barco se le voltió
pero ese humito sagrado
a nosotros nos salvó
le agradezco a la cultura
y al indio que la sombró

Yo nunca he tenido pleito
con los Koreanos del norte
el gobeirno entremétido
se mete aunque no le importe
y ahí voy yo como tarugo
ya es tiempo que me las corte

Ya no se anden enlistando
les digo yo a mis carnales
de que sirven las medallas
si nos ven como animales
ahí les dejo sus bisteques
yo prefiero mis nopales

Ya con ésta me despido
con respeto al ancho mar
no pierdo las esperanzas
de volverlo a nevegar
pero en un buque Chicano
con la bandera de Aztlán

EL ROSINANTE

Yo tengo mi Rosinante
que apenitas puede andar
rueda un poco pa' delante
yo lo demás para atrás

¡Ay! Pero cuando su pito pita
El Rosinante no se agüita
da un volido pa' adelante
y no lo puedo parar

Yo le compro gas del caro
porque es muy particular
cuando le echo del barato
se amacha y no quiere andar

¡Ay! Pero cuando su pito pita
El Rosinante no se agüita
se me suelta retozando
y hasta quema regular

Los chotas ya lo conocen
porque es muy agitador
le han dao tickets en Delano
y trae baleado el rayador

¡Ay! Pero cuando su pito pita
El Rosinante no se agüita
el se pone al pie de lucha
a hacerle huelga al City Hall

Los topes con los molinos
la bateria le han bajao
las brecas no lo detienen
ya ni fenders le han quedao

¡Ay! Pero cuando su pito pita
El Rosinante no se agüita
se convierte en un low rider
y sin hydraulics va a brincar

En un viaje pa' Coachella
una troquita se encontró
y por andar puchando trocas
el mofle se le cayó

¡Ay! Pero cuando su pito pita
El Rosinante no se agüita
se juyó con su troquita
y hasta el mofle olvidó

La plebe de Aeronaves
cuando lo miran llegar
ya saben que viene crudo
y que se viene a curar

¡Ay! Pero cuando su pito pita
El Rosinante no se agüita
de volada hace coleta
pa' trae algo que pistiar

Ya con ésta me despido
hay que ir a desensillar
porque la lucha es muy larga
no nos queremos quemar

Porque la lucha es muy larga
¡Pero la vamos a ganar!

CRUZIN'

It's not the Boardwalk
in Santa Cruz
it's not a stroll down
in Malibu
we just cruzin', oh yea
we just cruzin'

It's not the Sunset
in Hollywood
we just go cruzin'
in our nieghborhood
we go cruzin', oh yea
we go cruzin'

BIG MOMMA

Take a look at poor Momma
don't seem like she's gonna
be able to take it
much longer, my friend

She's as tough as she's tender
and she won't surrender
but all of them blows
they are taken their toll

Now Momma can take it
but she ain't gonna fake it
and if she gonna make it
it's up to you and I

We got to watch them ambitious
sons of the witches
and which is the way
they would like to see her go

It ain't proper to drop her
when she's on her knees
rally 'round sons and daughters
get her up on her feet

We got to make an assessment
protect our investment
show dear old Momma
she didn't raise a bunch of fools

Now it ain't about nations
what it's about is her patience
rally 'round all you Razas
from all four directions (bis)

PESADILLA YANQUI

Hermano nicaragüense
hermano salvadoreño
escucha el clamor chicano
que te canta un carnal aztleño
Desde las tierras meshicas
hasta la punta de Chile
de las nieves alasqueñas
a las islas del Caribe
En Aztlán como en Puerto Rico
y también en Panamá
llevamos el mismo sueño
de encontrar la libertad

Pero hay una pesadilla
que nos roba la unidad
pa' que ese sueño precioso
se nos pueda realizar

Porque hay una pesadilla
que nos roba la unidad
y de ese mal sueño yanqui
es tiempo de despertar (bis)

ARPA CHICANA

Si mi arpa Chicana
les pudiera hablar
les contara de amores bonitos
de cosas re chulas
antes de harcerlos llorar

Y ese llanto ha de ser de alegría y
el orgullo de ser mexicano
porque esa sangre de indio
que nunca se a rajado
también está de este lado

Porque en Aztlán como en Tenochtitlán
desde por acá hasta la Tierra del Fuego
de este lado de un mar muy profundo
ya mi gente tenía su mundo

Pero de que me sirve ser tan mexicano
si no respeto a mi hermano el chicano
y de que me sirve ser ta' re-chicano
si cada día me niego que soy mexicano

Porque en Aztlán como en Tenochtitlán
desde por acá hasta la Tierra del Fuego
De este lado de un mar muy profundo
ya mi gente tenía su mundo

EL TIRILONGO

Le dicían El Tirilongo
chicano azteca, hijo del sol
le gustaba borlotear
le gustaba colorear
le gustaba ver el sol
pa' los mambos y pa'l boogie
el tachuachito y el patín
al Tirilongo Tirili
le dicían El Machine

Le decían el Tirilongo
indio-hispano hijo del sol
le gustaba borlotear
le gustaba peregrinar
le gustaba ver el sol
pa' las rumbas y los tangos
el famenco y el patín
al Tirilongo Tirili
le decían El Gypsy King

Le decían el Tirilongo
chicano azteca, hijo del sol
Le gustaba borlotear
le gustaba colorear
le gustaba ver el sol

Le decían el Tirilongo
cholo apache hijo del sol
le gustaba borlotear
le gustaba tamborear
le gustaba ver el sol
en el Sun Dance y en los Pow-Pows
danzas azteca y el patín
al Tirilongo Tirili

Le decían El Matachin

CHICANOS EN KOREA

Ay, aztlan del corazón
Tierra antigua de mi gente
Porque nos tratan tan mal
Como hijos desobedientes.
Somos indios mexicanos,
Sin embargo somos gente.

Año del cincuenta y uno
En el condado de Fresno
Se compadecio un juez
Y hasta me paso quebrada,
Seis meses en el tabique
¿O cuatro años en la armada?

En un buque me encontré
Al Beto del Paso, Texas
Me ofreció la beinvenida
Y unos toques de su tecla
Me dice aquí no hay fijón
Aquí la tenemos hecha.

Me dice soy veterano
Artillero de primera
Y esa cinco trienta y ocho
Esa es mi fiel compañera
Y contigo en mi cuadrilla
Le atizamos a cualquiera.

Sabes que le dije yo,
Gracias por tus intenciones
Pero es que a mí por derecho
Me caen sura los cañones.
Sé cura y le da a la bacha
Los últimos jalones.

No fijeishen no notation
Me asegura el artillero
Yo sé que eres vato loco
Y no cualquier marinero
Cuando empiezen los plomazos
Allí en la torre te espero.

El capitán era un ruco
Que le gustaba pistiar
Oficiales verdolagas
Le tenían escame al mar
'Pos nosotros muy cochudos
En la pocar y el conquian.

Navegamos a Japón
Y yo no hablaba en japonés
Me lo enseñó una chaparra
Al derecho y al revés
Siendo un vato agradecido
Le enseñé a darse las tres.

En un congal muy famoso
En el puerto de Yokuska
Donde iba toda la plebe
A vacilar con las rucas
Y a bailar un mambo o dos
Y acordarse de sus chucas.

Los chicanos en Korea
Se portaron con honor
Ganaron muchas medallas
Hasta liberty en Japón
Pero al volver al cantón
Derechito a la prisión.

Ay, aztlán del corazón
Tierra antigua de mi gente
Por qué nos tratan tan mal
Como hijos desobedientes
Somos indios mexicanos
Sin embargo
Somos gente.

EL BILLY BILLY MILITANTE

El Billy Billy Militante
Came to the varrio
Riding a jeep
Going bleep bleep bleep.
Within a matter of time
They had him on a track
And the brotha never did
Come back.

El Billy Billy y la Millie
Se iban a casar
When they heard the sounds
Going ra za saz.
It was never determined
What exactly came down
'Cept that Billy never came
Back to town.

Now Billy talks to Millie
In that shadow world of fear.
What he tells her doesn't
Make much sense but it's exactly
What she wants to hear.

El Billy Billy y la Millie
Se iban a casar
When they heard the sounds
Going ra za saz.

It was never determined
What exactly came down
'Cept that Billy never came
Back to town.

Now Millie talks to Billy
In that shadow world of fear.
What she tells him doesn't
Make much sense but it's exactly
What he wants to hear.

Acknowledgements Continued

El Espejo The Mirror, edited by Octavio I. Romano-V, 1969, Quinto Sol Publications, Inc., P.O. Box 9275, Berkeley, CA 94709
El Pobre Viejo Walt Whitman
El Vendido
Sunstruck While Chopping Cotton
Lazy Skin
In a Pink Bubble-Gum World
Los Vatos
La Jefita
Resonant Valley

Mark in Time, Portraits and Poetry/San Francisco, 1971, Glide Publications, 330 Ellis St., San Francisco, CA 94102
Forgive?

Literatura Chicana texto y contexto, Chicano Literature text and context, 1972, Prentice Hall, Inc., NJ
El Louie

El Sol y Los De Abajo and other R.C.A.F. poems por José Montoya, 1972, dibujo by Armando Cid, Ediciones Pocho-che, San Franscisco, CA
Early Pieces
Gabby Took The 99
This Valley in September
"Jesse"
Misa en Fowler
From '67 to '71
The Hour Is Today
Valor y Locura
Jack-Off Hangover
Irish Priests And Chicano Sinners
Rabia
Esque Se Va Morir Don Chema
Morir de Susto
Summer Soon Sunday Afternoon
My My!
Los Campos De Corcoran
Xmas '71
Monterey
Oh y Oh
Torres
S Street Y La Cinco Del Barrio

La Muerte de un Gato
El Sol y Los de Abajo
A Moco Pome

Aztlan, an Anthology of Mexican American Literature, edited by Luis Valdez and Stan Steiner, 1972, Random House, Inc. New York, NY
El Louie, La Jefita

Time To Greez, Introduction by Maya Angelou, 1975, Glide Publications, Third World Communications, 330 Ellis Street, San Francisco, CA 94102
Don't Ever Lose Your Driver's License
Barrio Landmark

Grito Del Sol, A Chicano Quarterly, Canto Al Pueblo, 1978, Edited by Octavio Romano-V Tonatiuh International Inc., Publishers, 2150 Shattuck, Berkeley, CA
Until They Leave Us A Loan

Calafia, The California Poetry, project director Ishmael Reed, 1979 Y'Bird, 2140 Shattuck Ave, Rm. 311, Berkeley, CA 94704
Gabby Took The 99
From '67 to '71

Chicanos, Antología Histórica y Literaría, 1980, Fondo de Cultura Economica, Avenida de la Universidad, 975, Mexico 12, D.F.
Se Fue Ricardo
El Barrio en Enero
Faltan Quince pa' las Cuarto
Soledad
New Blood Magazine, 1982, New Blood Press, 2935 Broadway, Boulder, CO 80302
Los Theys Are Us

Fiesta In Aztlan, Anthology of Chicano Poetry, edited by Toni Empringham, 1982, Capra Press, P.O. Box 2068, Santa Barbara, CA 93120
El Louie

Imagine, International Chicano Poetry Journal, Special Issue, Winter 1984, Imagine Publishers, 645

Beacon St., Suite 7, Boston, MA 02215
The Telling Signs of Downtown
How Great Was My Valley

Landing Signals, An Anthology of Sacramento Poets, edited by Douglas Blazek, Ann Menebroker, C.K. Dobbs, 1985, the Sacramento Poetry Center Sierra 2, 2791 24th Street, #8, Sacramento, CA 96818
They Sent Men To Match Mountains

Erlanger Studien, Contemporary Chicano Poetry, An Anthology, edited by Wolfgang Binder, 1986, West Germany
Pobre Viejo Walt Whitman
Sunstruck While Chopping Cotton
El Louie
Los Vatos
La Jefita

The Trilogy Poems, Part One VOCES, An Anthology of Nuevo Mexicano Writers, 1987, El Norte Publications, P.O. Box 7266, Albuquerque, NM 87194
La Yarda De La Escuelita
La Jefita

Watch From The Sky, 1988, Pinyon Press, 2738-4th Ave. Alley, Sacramento, CA 95818
How Great Was My Valley

The Maverick Poets, An Anthology, edited by Steve Somit, 1988, Gorilla Press, 9269 Mission Gorge Road, Suite 229, Santee, CA 92071
Metamorphosis
Five Alone
Listen

Quarry West 26, Chicanas y Chicanos en Diálogo, edited by Francisco Alarcón and Lorna Dee Cervantes, 1989, Quarry West, Porter College, University of California, Santa Cruz, CA 95064
Barrio Landmark
Una Lagrima por tu Amor

Inconclusionist: Sacramento Voices, A Commemorative Anthology for 3 Universes in the Atomic Cafe,
I.D.E.A. Gallery, 1990, edited by Margret Boone and Bea Herrera, Boonwood Publishing, Sacramento, CA
The Dog Dreamers

An Ear to the Ground, An Anthology of Contemporary American Poetry, 1989 edited by Marie Harris and Kathleen Aguero, University of Georgia Press, Athens, GA, 30602
Rough Time in th' Barrio

Puerto Del Sol, Vol. 27, No.1, Spring 1992, Special Edition, Jim Sangel, University of New Mexico, Los Cruses, NM
Pachuco Portfolio

Vol. 27, No. 1, Spring '92, Special Issue, edited by Jim Sagel, University of New Mexico, Las Cruces, New Mexico.
Pachuco Portfolio

Trio Casindio and the Royal Chicano Air Force, 20 Years of Songs by José Montoya.
Garbanzo Beret, 1971
Lulac Cadillac, 1972
Los Huelguistas, 1973
Chicanos en Korea, 1978
Marinero Mariguano, 1978
Derelict Dawg, 1978
El Rosinante, 1979
Cruzin, 1983
Big Momma, 1984
Pesadilla Yanqui, 1984
El Billy Billy Militante, 1988
Harpa Chicano, 1988
El Tirilongo, 1990

Some of these songs appeared on the album, CHICANO MUSIC ALL DAY, produced by El Instituto de Lengua y Cultura, P.O. Box 6, Elmira, CA 95625